The Phantom of the Opera

A Musical Play

Book and Lyrics by Ken Hill

Arrangements and Incidental Music
by Alasdair MacNeill

Music by Offenbach, Gounod, Verdi, Boito, Dvořák,
Bizet,Weber, Donizetti, Mozart

Based on the novel by Gaston Leroux

Samuel French — London
New York - Toronto - Hollywood

ISBN 978 0 573 08096 8

THE PHANTOM OF THE OPERA

The Phantom of the Opera by Ken Hill, based upon the novel by Gaston Leroux, was presented at the Shaftesbury Theatre from 18th December 1991. The cast was as follows:

Jammes	Kate Harbour
Richard	Reginald Marsh
Rémy	Gary Lyons
Debienne	Richard Tate
Raoul	Steven Pacey
Mephistopheles	Haluk Bilginer
Faust	Michael McLean
1st Stage Hand	Quentin MacLaine
Madam Giry	Toni Palmer
Christine Daaé	Christina Collier
La Carlotta	Tracie Elisabeth Gillman
The Phantom	Peter Straker
Lady in Box	Jacqueline Barron
The Groom	Richard Tate
The Gravedigger	Richard Tate
Lisette	Jacqueline Barron
2nd Stage Hand	Richard Shilling
The Old Man	Richard Tate
Dominique	Tracie Elisabeth Gillman
The Persian	Haluk Bilginer
Mauclair	Richard Tate
The Chorus Girl	Tracie Elisabeth Gillman
The Priest	Richard Tate

Directed by Ken Hill
Assistant Director Peter Rankin
Musical Direction by Alasdair MacNeill
Designed by Sarah-Jane McClelland
Lighting Design by Gerry Jenkinson
Sound Design by Clem Rawlings

The Phantom of the Opera by Ken Hill, based upon the novel by Gaston Leroux, received its first public performance in a production by the Duke's Playhouse Lancaster, 26th July 1976. It was directed by John Blackmore, designed by Clare Lyth, with musical direction by Gary Yershon. It differed from later versions in having a modern score in addition to excerpts from *Faust* by Charles Gounod.

The Phantom of the Opera was also produced in a joint production by the Newcastle Playhouse and the Theatre Royal, Stratford East, on 3rd April 1984. Alasdair MacNeill arranged all the music and composed all the incidental music for this production. The modern score was discarded, and all airs were taken from opera. The cast on that occasion was as follows:

Jammes	Lynn Schofield
Richard	Gordon Reid
Rémy	Gary Lyons
Debienne	Ron Emslie
Mephistopheles	Haluk Bilginer
Faust	John Aron
Stage Hand	Stage managment
Madam Giry	Toni Palmer
Christine Daaé	Christina Collier
La Carlotta	Franchine Mulrooney
The Phantom	Peter Straker
Lady in Box	Stage management
The Groom	Ron Emslie
The Gravedigger	Ron Emslie
Lisette	Stage management
The Old Man	Ron Emslie
Dominique	Franchine Mulrooney
The Persian	Haluk Bilginer
Mauclair	Ron Emslie
The Chorus Girl	Franchine Mulrooney
The Priest	Ron Emslie

Directed by Ken Hill
Assistant Director Peter Rankin
Musical Direction by Alasdair MacNeill
Designed by Sarah-Jane McClelland

For Johnny Reinis

SYNOPSIS OF SCENES AND MUSICAL NUMBERS

ACT I

ACT II

MUSIC SOURCES

Song 1	"Jamais, foi de Cicerone" from *La Vie Parisienne* by Jacques Offenbach
Song 2	"Maudites soyez-vous" from *Faust* by Charles Gounod
Song 3	"O inferno! Amelia qui!" from *Simon Boccanegra* by Giuseppe Verdi
Song 4	"Son lo spirito che nega" from *Mefistofele* by Arrigo Boito
Song 5	"Měsíčku na nebi hlubokém" from *Rusalka* by Antonín Dvořák
Song 6	"Je crois entendre encore" from *Les Pêcheurs de Perles* by Georges Bizet
Song 7	"A Paris nous arrivons en masse" from *La Vie Parisienne* by Jacques Offenbach
Song 8	"Que vois-je là?" from *Faust* by Charles Gounod
Song 9	"Adieu! Je ne veux pas te suivre, Fantôme" from *Les Contes d'Hoffmann* by Jacques Offenbach
Song 10	"Ah! C'est la voix!" from *Faust* by Charles Gounod
Song 11	"Du weißt daß, meine Frist" from *Der Freischütz* by Carl Maria von Weber, and "Rè dell'abisso, affrettati" from *Un Ballo in Maschera* by Giuseppe Verdi
Song 12	"Non so le tetre immagini" from *Il Corsaro* by Giuseppe Verdi
Song 13	"Mentre gonfiarsi l'anima" from *Attila* by Giuseppe Verdi
Song 14	"Deserto sulla terra" from *Il Trovatore* by Giuseppe Verdi
Song 15	"Chi mi frena in tal momento" from *Lucia di Lammermoor* by Gaetano Donizetti
Song 16	"Avant de quitter ces lieux" from *Faust* by Charles Gounod
Song 17	Reprise of Song 16
Song 18	"Alla vita è sempre ugual" from *Don Giovanni* by Wolfgang Amadeus Mozart

PRODUCTION NOTE

The playing should be real and controlled, stretched to the limits of what is believable, but never beyond. 'Camping' or 'guying' is not permitted. The characters are somewhat thinly drawn, but must be fleshed out with the actor's own personality, and played truthfully. Playing for laughs will destroy the story. The narrative is gripping, and relies heavily on atmosphere and thrills. Where there is comedy in a scene, it should be thrown away deftly, dead-pan, almost as if it were unimportant. Grasping this simple, yet rather delicate style, will be the difference between good and bad theatre, success and failure.

The setting must be designed to permit fast, fluid action, with the maximum of effect created with the minimum of fuss. There are no scene changes as such. A short black-out, a few chords of music, and we are on into the next scene. The rhythm of the play demands the approach. Anything more cumbersome will not only make it very long, it will reduce its impact and lessen its tension.

For convenience, the script describes the setting used in the later productions, designed by Sarah-Jane McClelland.

For all scenes taking place in the auditorium and on the stage of the Opera House, a red tableau curtain was flown in behind a decorated front portal representing the Paris Opera House. At the same time, two small, decorated boxes were trucked in from right and left. When used, the curtain was drawn up in classical tableau style. The centre split was an important entrance.

For scenes not taking place in the auditorium or on the stage, the tableau curtains were flown out fully, and the boxes trucked off. Something approximating this device is necessary, since it is important the audience understand when they are participating in a performance at the Paris Opera House, and when they are watching a scene from The Phantom of the Opera.

The chandelier can be the house chandelier, if one exists and if access is permitted. Only a small movement will, of course, be allowed. By far the more spectacular was a large prop chandelier in the auditorium, which could be swung alarmingly. Whichever is used, it is very important the chandelier is over the heads of some of the audience, and that as many as possible can see it.

Immediately behind the tableau curtains was flown a painted cloth, depicting, in a general sense, a corridor in the Opera House. This permits most upstage scenes to be preset.

Hinged forward in the entrances left by the trucked boxes right and left were two door-frames, that on the right containing a barred gate, that on the left a non-practical door to a dressing room, which was replaced with a similar barred gate in the interval.

Upstage there was a second portal, of a similar but muted design, able to work pictorially in both 'opera' and 'non-opera' scenes. Both portals contained sets of sconces, those on the first portal practical, those on the second not.

Behind the second portal were flown three painted cloths and a simple black masking cloth. All the painted cloths were designed for back-lighting and represented, as follows:

(i)   An all purpose 'Faust' cloth used in all the 'Faust' opera scenes. It was highly-coloured, a medieval devil swallowing the world.

(ii)   A 'Forest' cloth for use in Act II, Scene 7. A primitive jungle, containing some animals and blue sky, highly coloured.

(iii)   An 'Organ' cloth for use in the play's last scene. Purple pipes, painted three-dimensional in perspective, appeared to emanate from the keyboard butted up to it.

At the rear, as deep as possible was a black star-cloth. The stars are only used in one scene (the roof) and for all other scenes where the second portal is open, all is black and void. Even scenes where a sky might be expected, for example, the Office, had a black background. The floor was black and shiny.

At all times, action was contained 'within' the setting in which curtain or cloth rose. The downstage area was used only for downstage scenes in the Opera House, or before the 'corridor' cloth. The only exception to this rule was the occasional spill permitted in the Boiler Room, the Bottom Cellar and the Chapel.

Finally, included as part of the permanent setting, were two drop-boxes, right, one containing sawdust, the other the Phantom's prayer-book.

Costumes

The true period of the story is late nineteenth century, but the costumes reflected a slightly later period, after the turn of the century, which produces a nicer line, especially for Christine.

Pronunciation

There are no *M'sieurs* or *Mamselles* in this play. They translate perfectly properly as Mr and Miss, as in real life. Madam is retained, however, for Madam Giry, since it seems more of a title, and adds colour to the character. The pronunciation, however, is English and not M*adame*.

The dialogue is standard English, but pronunciation of French proper names should be correct, though not heavily accented. For example: Ric-*hard*, Chris-*tine*. The 'J' of Jammes and 'G' of Giry are soft.

Singing

At first sight, the score may appear rather daunting. However, it is important to realize that in most cases the airs from opera are used for musical comedy purposes. Only Faust and Christine need to convince as opera-singers. The Phantom, by his very nature, needs to reach across and 'touch' us. A more modern voice is best here, then — even high rock. Raoul, the Persian and Madam Giry need to be better than average, but the rest need only good actor 'character' voices. The range called for by Madam Giry is rather extreme, and some passages in the sextet might best be doubled off for her.

ACT I
SCENE 1

Under New Management

The stage and auditorium of the Paris Opera House at the turn of the nineteenth century

The boxes are on stage, the curtains are closed, the chandelier and the House Lights are on. On cue, a quiet sinister drone creeps in under audience chatter. Once established, House Lights and stage Lights fade to Black-out. In this, the CURTAIN *opens. A long shaft of "working light" builds along the floor from* UL, *followed by a dim acting area.* UC, *below the second portal, is a very tall pair of wooden step-ladders, the 'A' shape facing the audience. Beyond, in the blackness, there are a couple of paint-spattered chairs with pots of paint and brushes lying about*

After a moment, Jammes enters from UL, *crossing behind the ladder to* UR, *on her way out after a long rehearsal. She is a pretty, teenage ballet dancer, wearing a practise skirt and shawl, carrying a reticule, her black hair done up in a neat bun. As she passes the ladder* R, *she becomes aware that the stage and auditorium is empty, and pauses to peer out. Seeing no-one, she runs to* C. *There is still nobody about. Delighted, she tosses her shawl and reticule off* R, *moves back to* C, *strikes a pose, and begins to dance. The dance becomes a set of pose turns, travelling to* DL, *where the last one goes wrong, and she falls over. Her muttered 'shit!' is well audible but she rises to smile prettily and continue. She finishes in a low pose* R. *As she does so, a white rose is tossed from high above to land before her. Big sting in the music. She picks the rose up and turns quickly to peer off* R. *Another big sting. Slowly she lifts her eyes, higher and higher, the music building, until she is pointing almost straight up to where the rose came from*

Jammes (*screaming*) It's him! It's him! He's been watching me!

Screaming, she runs off L, *her screams taken up by other girls, fading away down corridors. The music stops except for a thin sound of strings. A lengthy pause, then a sudden high-pitched giggling cry is heard from the rear of the auditorium, hopefully making people jump. It is from Rémy, who can be seen blundering down an aisle,* L, *followed by Richard. Richard is in a coat and top-hat, carrying a cane. Rémy carries a ledger and pencil. He wears glasses*

Richard (*irritably*) What is it, Rémy?

Rémy I banged my nose on this pillar, sir. It's so dark in here.

Richard Why don't they turn on some lights? I'm the new manager of the Paris Opera House, not a bloody owl.

Rémy I did tell Mr Debienne we were coming, sir.

Richard Not loudly enough, it seems. Now come here.

Rémy What about my nose?

Richard Bring it with you. (*He climbs steps up onto the stage,* L) This is intolerable. It's my first day here, and I'm being completely ignored. You're my secretary, Rémy, do something!

Rémy (*clambering up steps*) How many steps are there, sir?

Richard I think there are five.

Crash and yell from Rémy

Six. Now get up, and turn on some light!

Bright lights build, revealing Richard standing and Rémy lying flat, extreme DL

Well done, Rémy. You see how easy it is when you try?

Debienne drags Jammes on from L, *crossing to* R

Debienne (*to her*) Come on, you silly girl. We've turned the stage lights on for you, there's no need to be frightened. (*He pushes her in front of him, and indicates above*) There you are — nothing.

Richard and Rémy ease UL *trying to see what he's talking about*

And don't spread silly rumours. There's a new manager due, and he's a pompous old —

Richard Debienne!

Debienne (*spinning round*) Good Lord, I'm awfully sorry, sir. We were expecting you later.

Richard That's quite obvious. (*He indicates Jammes*) Now what's all this about?

Jammes (*leaping up and down, doing entrechats in her excitement, pointing*) I saw him, sir, I saw him! Clear as anything!

Richard Saw who? What is she talking about?

Debienne (*quickly*) Nothing, sir. Imagination. Allow me to present Miss Jammes — a member of our Corps de Ballet. (*To her, with meaning*) Mr Richard — our new *manager*.

Jammes Oh, shi—

Debienne claps a hand to her mouth, spins her into a pirouette, and she bows, low

Debienne (*presenting her*) She says, hallo.

Richard Get up, girl, get up. I hate fuss. In my previous capacity as President of the Northern Railways, I had it eradicated entirely. (*He looks about*) And where's my son? (*To Debienne, accusingly*) We've lost my son.

All move about the stage, looking for him

Raoul!

Raoul (*in the auditorium,* R) Just taking a dekko at the auditorium, Dad. No need to panic.

He runs up steps R onto the stage, and crosses to C, a good-looking if slightly daft young man, wearing a hat and coat, with a white rose in his button hole, carrying a cane

Splendid, isn't it?

All move back downstage to peer out front

Richard (*dubiously*) Some of it.

Raoul backs upstage during the following, and continues his exploration off R, *to reappear in Box Six, where he takes off his hat and leaves it, together with his cane. He smiles on Jammes who sits against the box doing exercises. Throughout the play, she is never still*

Personally, I've always thought of the Paris Opera House as being more — more —

Rémy Bigger, sir?

Richard Quiet, Rémy. (*To Debienne*) Debienne, why isn't it more ... bigger?

Debienne (*snatching at anything*) It's the lighting, sir. Our man Mauclair turns on the gas, and the whole place is transformed.

Rémy Yes, and speaking of lighting, Mr Debienne, that chandelier doesn't look too secure.

Richard I shan't tell you again, Rémy. (*To Debienne*) Debienne, that chandelier doesn't look too secure.

Debienne (*desperately trying to remember when he last had it checked*) Well, I hope it is, sir. Must weigh half a tonne.

Richard Precisely. What if it were to fall down?

Debienne (*incredulous*) Fall down? Our chandelier? (*After a beat, he points*) What, you mean on those seats there?

Richard (*pointing with cane*) Yes, and possibly there — and there — or even there.

Brief pause, having thoroughly alarmed anybody sitting underneath the chandelier

Rémy Well, the cheap seats will be safe.

All turn to glare at him

Faust (*singing off, L*)
                             Appear, Satan!
                             Appear!

Richard and Debienne break R, Rémy DL a little, looking about them

Mephistopheles (*singing off, L*) I am —

He swings on a rope to land up LC

— here!

He struts down LC *to strike a menacing masculine pose. He is dressed as a traditional red devil in doublet, hose, boots, horns, black beard, moustache and long tail*

Richard (*staring*) Who the devil are you?
Debienne (*quickly*) Well spotted, sir. It *is* the Devil. Mephistopheles, actually — rehearsing for tonight's performance of *Faust* (*To Mephistopheles, behind Richard's back, indicating him carefully*) Mr Richard — our new Manager.
Mephistopheles (*camp*) Oh! Enchanted!

He tries to take Richard's hand, but Richard isn't having any of it

D'you like the new entrance? The producer wants me to make this sudden, surprise, supernatural out-of-the air-from-nowhere appearance (*turning to Rémy*) and I think it's rather good.

He moves back to the rope, handing it off to a stagehand and meets Faust who enters from L, *wearing his dressing gown — a plump, pompous tenor*

Rémy Incidentally, who's singing Faust this evening?
Faust I am. (*He moves down*) I always sing Faust. (*He holds out his hand to Richard*) I only sing Faust.
Richard (*going to take his hand*) Well, I hope you sing it well.
Faust (*withdrawing his hand, offended*) Sing it well? Of course I sing it well. *I'm* singing it, aren't I?
Debienne (*hurrying* DC) We all sing well here, sir. In fact, we've prepared a little musical (*he claps his hands to orchestra*) introduction for you.

With squeals of delight, Faust, Mephistopheles and Jammes join Rémy DL *to form a tight little group, Jammes kneeling at the front and hitting her pose instantly at the end of the introduction. Debienne moves a little up* LC

Song 1: Welcome, Sir, I'm So Delighted

Debienne   Welcome, sir, I'm, so delighted
                           Everyone is so excited

He indicates the group, who give Richard little flutters with their fingers

What we need is someone new —just like you
To pull this sinking ship back into shape
(*To front*) And then we might forget the very dreadful
    way
That really awful things go on here every day

There has been agitation in the ranks at this. Rémy steps a little DL, rapping his ledger with his pencil. Faust and Mephistopheles cross to be behind Debienne, one to each ear

Rémy   That's quite enough of that
Faust   ⎱ (*together; to each other, lifting Debienne*)
Mephistopheles ⎰ You're not supposed to rat
Debienne (*spreading his hands*) Slipped out
Faust   ⎱
Mephistopheles ⎰ (*together; to each other*) No doubt

They drop him and Rémy crosses to Richard, who has eased over to the box to be with Raoul

Rémy (*to Richard*) Ignore him, dear sir
Richard   A word, if I may
                           I've something to say

Faust and Mephistopheles have broken upstage a little and are whispering together

Rémy (*to them*)   Pay attention, there!
                        (*to Jammes, indicating off* L) Close that door!

As Jammes hurries round Debienne, Faust and Mephistopheles, to disappear off UL, *Rémy is singing off into the wings* R

                        Let's have some silence here — not a sound!

Faust and Mephistopheles rejoin Debienne who is cupping his hands to his ears. They sing to Richard

Debienne ⎫
Faust ⎬ (*together*) We're all agog, sir.
Mephistopheles ⎭
Richard (*using his cane to indicate an area* DR)
          Gather round

In a little musical break, Richard crosses to L, *Raoul leaves the box, Debienne, Rémy, Faust and Mephistopheles form a little group* DR, *Debienne and Rémy at the rear, Jammes dancing back on once more to take a low position at the front of them, hitting her pose instantly at the end of the break*

                    I'd like to say—

Raoul re-enters quickly from R, *and crosses to Richard*

Raoul   We'd like to say
                    (*To Richard*) Include me, too
                    Unless you feel
                    I'm in the way
Richard (*irritated*) Not at all
                    But let me speak

He crosses L *a little, as the chastened Raoul breaks upstage a little*

Mephistopheles (*aside, to the others*)
                    He's very chic
                    It's unique

Faust crosses to C

Faust (*to Richard; ingratiatingly*)
                    We're at your service
                    Devotedly
                    We're waiting with bated breath
                    Your loyal troops
                    (*He indicates they should lift on to their toes*)
                    Especially me

*He indicates they can drop down again. In the small break that follows,
Jammes dances R a little, and presents her group. In all that follows, which
is a simple, fairly static setting based upon three groups: Faust, Mephistopheles; Debienne, Rémy; Richard, Raoul; Jammes, who does not sing,
fills every tiny moment with dance or movement*

Richard (*crossing back in a little*)
                        I want my staff
                        To be a team
                        To make me proud
                        To be their boss
Faust   We will, not half
Richard (*crossing back L angrily*)
                        Don't intervene
Raoul (*moving into Faust*)
                        It's not allowed
                        And makes him cross

*Seizing his opportunity, Mephistopheles leaves the group, delicately pulls
Faust back by the scruff of his neck, and takes his place*

Mephistopheles (*ingratiatingly; to Richard*)
                        I like your plan
                        So just say when
                        I'll help you pick
                        Your new recruits
Richard   Well done, that man
                        Ten out of ten
Faust (*to the others*)
                        She loves to lick
                        The boss's boots

Mephistopheles turns on him moving UR

Mephistopheles   You rotten beast
Faust   Get knotted, love
Mephistopheles   You amateur!
Faust   You're such a bitch
                        (*to Richard*) The true artiste

Is far above
This sort of gir—
——lishness

Mephistopheles   That's rich!

Debienne hurriedly pushes through them, crossing to c

Debienne   They understand you perfectly

Rémy pushes between them and joins Debienne, c

Rémy   Nobody here would disagree

During the following, Jammes moves behind them, takes them by the hand, comes between them, and kneels front once more in time to form their group for the chorus, acting the peace-maker. Amused by all this sycophancy, Raoul moves down to put his head between Debienne and Rémy and his hands on their shoulders

Raoul   And if they did, I'm sure they'd say (*He crosses to join his father*)

Debienne }   (*together; looking for him*)

Rémy }   Oh yes, they would, sir, right away

For the chorus, all face front, in three tight separate groups, Faust, Mephistopheles and Jammes R, *Rémy and Debienne* C, *and Raoul and Richard* L

All   We're a team from now on
United as one
We're all in perfect harmony

Rémy and Raoul break upstage, indicating Debienne and Richard

Debienne (*to Richard*)

May I say on behalf, sir
Of the artists (*he indicates them*) and staff, sir
(*He indicates himself*)
We would hope that you'd keep us all in your employ

Rémy (*crossing to put his head between Faust and Mephistopheles, hands on their shoulders*)
>They're so eager and loyal
>They'll pamper and spoil

Mephistopheles (*to Richard*)
>Any service at all, sir, call us

Faust (*nudging Jammes*)
>Don't be coy

Jammes gives Richard a little sexy wave

All (*except Richard*)
>Do, sir!
>We'll be happy to help you out
>Do, sir

Mephistopheles   Turn to me, if you can, sir
Richard   We shall see, we shall see
Raoul (*crossing to Debienne*)
>Don't count on it

He rejoins Richard, L, and the same three groups face front once more

All   It's the height of the season
>And the opera's the reason
>We are striving to see
>It's a stunning success

Jammes dances across to kneel c in front of Debienne and Rémy

>We'll regard it as treason
>If it's any less
>Tra la la la la la
>Mi mi mi mi!

During the following, Jammes indicates the singers, and uses hands and arms to bring the whole thing to a pretty finish

Debienne ⎫   (*together; to one another*)
Rémy   ⎬   What a hit it will be

Faust	You can leave it to me
Debienne ⎫	(*together; to Richard*)
Rémy ⎬	If you pay him his fee
Mephistopheles	Me, I'll do it for free
All	We're a team from now on
	United as one
	Everyone

They congratulate one another in ad-lib during any applause, Faust and Mephistopheles crossing to be near the box L, Jammes squatting before them, Rémy crossing DR, Raoul breaking UC to look off UR, Debienne shaking Richard's hand, C

Debienne Oh, well done, sir!

Richard Yes, I knew singing in the Stock Exchange Choir would come in handy one day. (*He crosses below Debienne to UR, joined by Rémy on his L*) Good luck for tonight.

Debienne (*quickly keeping level with him, UC*) Erm — there is one tiny fly in our ointment, sir. La Carlotta — our principal soprano ...

The group DL cast up their eyes, shake their heads

Richard What about her?

Debienne She's lost her voice.

Richard Jolly good.

He and Rémy turn to go R. They stop and do a take

What? (*He turns*) Lost —lost —?

Rémy Her voice, sir.

Richard Quiet, Rémy. (*He moves DR centre*) This is a catastrophe! The first performance under my management — cancelled!

Raoul (*hurrying down to his L*) No, Father, there's a new girl singing in Carlotta's place ... Christine Daaé.

Music. At the mention of the beautiful creature, all beam happily, Rémy putting his hands on the right side of his chest. Richard stares at them all

An admirable creature, with the most exquisite voice.

The music stops

Richard (*glaring at him*) Christine who?
Rémy Daaé, sir.
Debienne She's a — (*trying not to say it too loud*) — chorus girl, sir.
Richard A chorus girl?

Raoul glares at him, moving round him upstage, Debienne forced a little
UR

> Why wasn't I consulted? This is most improper. (*He crosses* L) Who
> decided that an unknown — a mere chorus girl — should take the place
> of the great Carlotta tonight? (*He drives Debienne back to Box Six*, R)
> Will somebody tell me? Well?
Madam Giry (*off*) It was the ghost ——

Music

> — sir.

The lighting checks a little

> *Madam Giry enters from* L, *crossing to* C, *and then moves straight*
> *downstage. She is tall and gaunt and glides on, dressed in a severe grey*
> *dress*

Richard Ghost? Did somebody say ghost?
Faust They did.

By now, she has moved down into Richard's eyeline, and Mephistopheles
moves in a little

Mephistopheles You've a lot to learn about this place, Mr Richard. (*To*
Madam Giry, waspish) We're a superstitious lot.
Madam Giry (*holding a hand to him but not looking at him*) Quiet! (*As*
Mephistopheles reacts) You'll upset (*looking up at the chandelier*) —
him!

Richard stares at her, stares at the chandelier, then turns to Debienne, his
voice cracking with incredulity

Richard Who the hell's this?

Debienne Madam Giry, sir — our Chief Box Keeper. She's been here ever since the theatre was built.

Richard (*to her*) You can't be serious! A ghost in the Opera House!

Madam Giry You'll find out soon enough. Why do you think the last manager left? He's got a lot of "pull" round here, has our ghost.

Richard Has he, indeed? Well, haunting us is one thing, recasting my operas is altogether too much, so tell him from me he's to watch it. (*He turns to go then turns back to her*) Oh, and incidentally, I shall be attending *Faust* this evening. Reserve me a box, will you. (*He indicates the box* L) That one will do.

Madam Giry (*horrified*) Box *Five*?

Music, underlaying all of the following is the 'Ghost' theme. Finding themselves near the dreadful place, Faust, Mephistopheles and Jammes shriek and scoot UC. *In the background, Raoul climbs the ladder to get a better look as Madam Giry crosses to Box Five, and lays a gloved hand on it*

I don't recommend it, sir.

Richard And why not, pray?

Madam Giry Box Five is reserved for the Ghost, sir. It's always been that way — ever since the Opera House was built.

Richard This 'Ghost' and his friends seem to have a well-oiled little racket going on here. (*He crosses to her*) Is there anything else we have to provide for 'him'?

Debienne Only his allowance, sir.

Richard His *what*?

Rémy (*crossing to him*) It's written into the lease, sir. Apparently, this Ghost is to receive an allowance of 20,000 francs a month.

Richard 20,000 francs a month! (*He forces him* UR) Who put that in the lease?

Madam Giry Nobody knows. When it was first drawn up, the clause just appeared — written in blood in a strange crabbed hand.

The music ends on a eerie scrape

Richard I see now why I was appointed to this place. The steadying hand that stamped out corruption in the Left Luggage Department of

Northern Railways is required, and I mean to start immediately. In the
meantime, I want *that* box— tonight — for *me*. Is that clear, Madam
Giry?
Madam Giry Oh yes, sir. But don't blame *me* for what happens.
Richard Ghosts, indeed! (*He crosses* UR) Come, Rémy. I've never heard
of anything so — so——
Rémy (*to Madam Giry, following him*) Outrageous!

They disappear, R

Madam Giry crosses a little, to C, *watching them*

Madam Giry He'll find out — just like the last one did.
Mephistopheles (*coming down to her* L) You and your spooks, Madam
Giry. You *are* a caution.
Madam Giry (*rounding on him, making him flinch back*) And *you*! (*She
turns back* R, *pointing at the others, sweeps round in a big circle to* UR)

The others all flinch back: Debienne to DR, *Faust and Jammes to* UC,
Raoul descends the ladder

You'll *all* find out. Just you wait ... and see.

Music, as she goes, L. *The music stops*

Debienne She has a point, my friend. Don't meddle.
Mephistopheles But I mean! Ghosts! There are no such things. (*He
crosses* DC *and calls out front*) You hear that, Phantom? You don't exist.

*He turns to go. It was all very casual. But the echoing, whispering voice
of the Phantom is heard in the auditorium*

The Phantom (*off, whispering*) You don't exist.

A pause. Jammes dances DR *to Debienne, Faust hurries* DL, *Raoul to up* LC,
all staring out front

Jammes What was that?
Raoul An echo — that's all.

Debienne Are you sure?
Faust (*to Mephistopheles*) It didn't sound like your voice.

Mephistopheles makes an angry gesture, draws himself up fully, stalks to
C, *and challenges the dark auditorium*

Mephistopheles You ... don't ... exist.

They all listen. There is a long—a very long—silence. Then Mephistoph-
eles makes a gesture of triumph, and turns to go. As he does so, the whisper
is heard again, louder, each word from a different part of the auditorium,
echoing

The Phantom (*off, whispering*) You ... don't ...exist.
Mephistopheles (*panicking*) What does he mean, I don't exist? I exist all
right! (*To Faust*) Feel me!

As Faust shrinks back, Mephistopheles turns to Debienne and Jammes

Feel me! (*As they shrink back*) Well, do I exist, or don't I?
Faust (*full of foreboding*) For the time being.

Music, as he goes, L

Raoul It *was* only an echo, you know.
Mephistopheles (*recovering*) Yes ... Yes, of course it was. (*He takes*
Jammes' hand) Come on, let's go to the bistro. (*As he leads her off,* L)
It's your turn to pay.

They go, L, *Jammes casting a look back at the dark auditorium, followed*
by Debienne. To Raoul's irritation, Debienne stops and looks back at the
chandelier. He comes DC, *considers it, holds up his hands, makes a*
whistling noise, drops his hands like a falling chandelier, and makes a
crashing noise. He considers the possibility of this, then dismisses it

Debienne (*to audience*) No—

He exits L

Raoul quickly checks that the coast is clear, runs DL, turns and holds out his arms

Raoul Christine!

Music. She runs on from R pausing a moment to look at him

They then run and meet C, to embrace. The music dies

Christine Oh, Raoul, if only your father didn't have this awful prejudice against chorus girls.
Raoul I think it's because Mother was one.
Christine But it's so unfair! Our love should be in the open, for all the world to envy.
Raoul Don't fret, dearest. After tonight you'll be famous, and everything will be different.
Christine Famous? I don't think so.
Raoul But everyone says your voice has improved amazingly.
Christine (*turning away, R*) Yes. Yes, it has.
Raoul (*worried*) What's the matter?
Christine (*dismissing whatever is on her mind and turning back to him*) Nothing. Nerves, I expect.

They go to kiss

Carlotta (*off*) Miss Daaé!
Raoul Dash!
Carlotta (*off*) Where is the girl?
Raoul Blast! We'd better not to be seen together.

He hurries to Box Six to pick up his hat and cane

Debienne (*off*) She's on stage.
Raoul I'll see you after the performance — to offer my congratulations.
Carlotta (*off*) Then get out of my way!

Raoul gives her his buttonhole — a white rose

Raoul Till then.

He hurries off, R

Debienne (*off*) But Madam Carlotta—
Carlotta (*off*) I tell you I wish to see this girl!

A slap, a cry from Debienne, and Carlotta, an imposing Spanish diva, carrying a distinctive fan, sweeps on to glare at Christine

So!
Debienne (*off*) Bitch.
Carlotta You are the little nobody who thinks to take the place of the great Carlotta? (*She flicks open her fan*)
Christine (*bobbing a curtsey*) No, madam, I wouldn't presume to do that.
Carlotta And yet I have heard a lot about this newly discovered voice of yours. What are you, a witch, that you can produce such an instrument from out of the air?
Christine I don't know, madam. It just seemed to happen.
Carlotta Well, listen to this. (*During the following, she moves in a circular manner, towards Christine, then to* L, *up and to* LC — *a precise position for what follows*) You may go on tonight — that is all. You cannot hope to be anything more than a disappointment. And afterwards, we shall see whether there is any more need of you. We're very over-staffed, they tell me. In fact, I make this prediction: the new manager here will feel he has too many mouths to feed, and decide to make some savings — beginning with *you.*

Behind her, the huge ladder has begun topple forwards

Christine Look out!

Carlotta turns as the ladder brushes her and crashes to the stage. It is worth making the point here that the ladder must fall very near Carlotta and must appear very dangerous. A pause whilst Carlotta recovers. She hurries up to peer into the darkness upstage, but there is nobody there — the ladder stood in the middle of an empty stage. She turns to Christine in fury

Carlotta You seem to have a lot of friends here, Miss Daaé! Well, so have I. (*She crosses* L) So have I!

She exits L

Christine runs to the ladder to stare down at it. Later, she will be unsure whether she heard anything

The Phantom (*off, whispering, echoing*) Chris— tine ...

She looks up and out quickly. Music crashes out, and the Lights fade quickly to Black-out, her white face the last thing we see. In the darkness the curtain falls in, the orchestra segué tuning-up sounds, and Light builds on:

SCENE 2

The First Performance

The stage and auditorium. Later that evening

The curtains are lit warmly, as are both boxes, the chandelier at a low level. Madam Giry enters Box Five from the rear

Madam Giry (*very disapproving*) Box Five, sir.

Richard enters from the rear

Richard There's no need to look so frightfully foreboding, Madam Giry — (*handing her his hat, cloak, etc.*) — nothing is going to happen.
Madam Giry No, sir. But when it does, I shall be over here.

She goes and Richard turns to see Rémy ushering a young lady into Box Six. All are in evening dress

Richard Good-evening, Rémy, Miss — erm —

Rémy coughs

Oh, I see. Fingers crossed, eh? Always a fraught moment when we put on — (*whispering*) — an understudy.

Raoul enters the box, handing off hat and gloves to Madam Giry

Ah, there you are. (*He sits and takes out a programme from a pocket in the box*) I do hope this Christine Daaé's going to be all right.

As Raoul sits, Madam Giry hands them both a pair of binoculars

Raoul Don't worry, Father. As soon as you hear her, you'll melt — just as I did.

Madam Giry casts up her eyes and goes

Richard opens his programme with a flourish

Richard (*with pride*) *Faust* by Charles Gounod ... (*He lowers his voice*) What's it about?
Raoul (*studying his own programme*) It's the well-known classic tale, Father.

Richard continues staring at Raoul

Oh, I see. Well, Faust, an old philosopher, sells his soul in exchange for youth and the love of the beautiful Marguerite. It begins with the old man cursing everything he once believed, and deciding to poison himself — the mortal sin that invokes the Devil. You saw the Devil practising his entrance earlier.
Richard That's what worries me.

The prelude begins and the Lights begin to fade

Managing the Opera House is one thing, but having to watch the wretched stuff ...
Raoul Quiet, it's beginning.

A little light remains on the two boxes as the curtain rises. At the rear, the glowing Faust cloth. Before it, a large ornate gothic chair and table, Faust — wearing a grey wig and a hooded cloak — slumped across it. He toys with his tomes, his scrolls, the skull of his mentor, rises, beats his brow,

*then advances on us to sing. Since he has a large tenor voice, all in the
boxes flinch back at his first note*

Song 2: Accursed All Base Pursuit of Earthly Pleasure

Faust   Accursed all base pursuit of earthly pleasure!
Accursed be the shackles binding me so cruelly to
    life
Accursed ye trinkets that entice me
(*He clasps the scrolls to his chest*)
Yet if I grasp them, fail to suffice me
(*He casts them down and snatches up a faded long-
    stemmed red rose, and sniffs it*)
Vain dreams of love, glory and strife
(*He kisses it and casts it aside*)
Breeding naught but dark despair
(*He assumes a despairing attitude* L, *then turns to
    snatch up a huge book*)
Accursed be science, faith in God, faith in prayer!
A curse on them all!
(*He throws down the book and lifts a blue poison
    bottle and goblet*)
Hear me, Satan!
(*He pours the bottle into the goblet in a big sweeping
    movement that shows it to be empty*)
On you I call!
(*He holds up the goblet, facing* L)
Appear!

Mephistopheles (*off*) I am he — aaagh!

He swings on from L, *but the rope is now a noose round his neck, and
he is choking. It is a strong swing and takes him fully off* R. *Richard,
Raoul and Rémy rise. As Mephistopheles begins a swing back, now
dead, Debienne pops his head on from* R

Richard Good God, what a terrible accident!
Raoul (*to Debienne, whispering loudly*) Bring down the curtain!

Debienne disappears

Meanwhile, the body has swung fully off L, and is beginning to swing back
R *again*

Richard (*to Rémy, whispering*) Quickly, Rémy, get a —
Rémy (*whispering loudly*) Doctor?
Faust (*crossing down to him, missing the body by a bit*) No! Fetch an understudy!

Rémy and the Lady leave Box Six

By now, the body is swinging back from off R to off L, pursued by Debienne

Richard (*to the audience*) Keep calm, everybody, keep calm.
Raoul (*whispering loudly*) They are keeping calm, Father.
Richard Then tell 'em to keep calmer!

Hanging onto Mephistopheles' legs, Debienne is dragged back on from L

Raoul (*to Debienne, whispering loudly*) Bring down the curtain!
Debienne (*whispering loudly*) We can't! The rope's caught in the pulley.
Richard (*whispering loudly*) Well, cut him down, then!

Richard and Raoul leave the box quickly. Rémy enters R, and assists in lowering the body to the floor, C

Debienne (*during this, shouting off R*) More light here! Where's Mauclair got to again? More gas!
Faust And where's that understudy? I was just warming up.
Debienne Oh, shut up!
Faust (*taking off the grey wig and beard in disgust*) I *have* been shut up! That's the problem.

Richard and Raoul hurry on from L, followed more slowly by Christine — in her peasant's costume — and Jammes — in her ballet costume — both just peering on from L. Gradually build bright light. Raoul kneels at the body, L, while Richard hurries downstage

Richard (*to audience*) So sorry, ladies and gentlemen. Be with you in a moment. (*He hurries up to Raoul's left*) How is he?

Raoul (*dropping Mephistopheles' hand*) He's rather dead, Father.

Faust faints into Debienne's arms

Rémy (*by the table* R, *peering up*) How on earth did it happen? It was safe enough this morning.

Debienne joins him, and now points at the body

Debienne Look! There's a note pinned to the body!
Richard By George, so there is! Rémy, what does it say?
Rémy (*kneeling quickly and reading*) "Pure Silk", sir.
Richard Not that one! (*He points*) That one! (*He casts up his hands*)
Rémy (*reading, puzzled*) "I don't exist".

Sting. Jammes goes on pointe

Faust (*hollow*) "I don't exist ..."

   He exits R

Christine Oh, no!

   She runs off, L

Raoul Christine, wait!

   He hurries after her

Debienne (*calling off,* R) Is that rope free yet?
Voice (*off*) Yes!
Rémy Then you can bring in the curtain!

Debienne is delicately lifting Mephistopheles' legs round so that they don't foul the curtain

Richard I'll give the orders here, Rémy. We have a crisis. Debienne, you may bring in the — erm —
Rémy (*warning him*) Curtain, sir.

They step smartly forward as it drops into place behind them

Richard (*to the audience*) I'm sorry to have kept you waiting, ladies and
gentlemen, but as you may be aware a small technical difficulty prevents
our continuing with this evening's performance of — the thing. We
shall, of course, replace the indisposed Mephi — Mephi —
Rémy —stopheles —
Richard —as soon as possible, and continue with the performance in a
few days time. I trust this is satisfactory.

*He turns to find that Madam Giry has entered through the side of the
curtain,* L *holding his hat and cloak. He recoils*

Ah! ... (*recovering*) What is it, Madam Giry?
Madam Giry I said I'd be here when nothing happened, sir.
Richard Give me those!

*He snatches the things from her, and begins his descent into the audito-
rium,* L *followed by Rémy*

As for you, Rémy, I want you to get onto the Coroner's —
Rémy Office?
Richard At once. I want this whole matter dealt with as soon as —
Rémy Possible?
Richard Right!

They leave the auditorium, watched sardonically by Madam Giry

*Music, as the lighting fades to Black-out. The boxes truck off, the door
flat* L *hinges closed, and the curtains fly out to reveal the "Corridor"
cloth. Music continues as Light builds on:*

SCENE 3

A Mysterious Conversation

Outside Christine's dressing-room. Same time

*The lighting is gloomy, a yellow light showing through the fan above the
door to the dressing-room, the sconces glowing dimly. Raoul hurries on
from* R

Raoul These damned corridors all look the same! (*He turns and looks back off the way he came*) Oh, Jammes — come here, quickly!

Jammes dances on, to land to his R

Can you help? I can't find Christine anywhere.
Jammes That's because she's in a star dressing-room tonight, sir — (*pointing with her toe*) — over there.
Raoul Of course. Thank you.

Jammes dances back off

Raoul approaches the door

The Phantom (*off*) Calm yourself, my dear, calm yourself.

Realizing Christine has someone with her, Raoul turns to leave

Christine (*off*) Why did it have to happen?
The Phantom (*off*) The poor fellow killed himself. It's no concern of ours.
Raoul (*pausing, puzzled*) Christine?

During the following, shadows flit across the fanlight and Raoul's face

Christine (*off*) Everything's ruined. I was going to sing tonight.
Raoul To whom does she speak?
The Phantom (*off*) There will be other nights. Carlotta's voice will not recover, I swear ... but you will sing only for me in future, Christine — only for me.
Raoul No!
Christine (*off*) Yes. I will sing only for you.
The Phantom (*off*) Then you will know that your soul is mine, and you must love me as only I can be loved. You will know that, Christine.
Christine (*off, a dead voice that fades, becoming an echo*) I will know that ... I will know that ... I will know that.

The Light in the fanlight goes out. The music underlay becomes piano only

Raoul The villain! Who is he? How dare she? (*He hammers at the door, tugging at the handle*) Christine! ... Open this door! ... Christine Daaé, you open this door this minute... *etc.*! (*He ad-libs*)

During this, the piano becomes louder and louder, more and more impassioned, Raoul casting glances over his shoulder at it, until finally he cracks and he strides DC to the pit

Oh, for God's sake, will you stop playing that bloody piano!

It stops

Thank you. Now can you please tell me, is there another way into Miss Daaé's dressing-room?
M.D. (*pointing right*) Through the chorus girls' room.
Raoul Thank you.

He crosses R then pauses

The chorus girls' room?

He whistles, and goes R

Fast fade to Black-out. Music, through which we hear the startled shrieks of the Chorus Girls. The "Corridor" cloth rises on:

SCENE 4

An Empty Room

Christine's dressing-room. Immediately following

Christine's dressing-room is dimly lit. At the rear, the second portal is filled with a piece containing a large mirror. To its right are a hat-stand with a garment hanging from it and a large potted plant. To the L, a small dressing-table and chair. On the floor, R, the crushed white rose given to her by Raoul. As the cloth flies out, Raoul hurries into the room from R

Raoul Christine! ... (*He stares about him*) Empty! She must have left while I ran round. I'll catch her.

He hurries off L

The lighting in the room checks sharply, building upstage of the mirror, and at the same time putting a little light on the door to Christine's dressing-room, still in position DL

Music, and we see the Phantom through the mirror as he runs forward to press himself flat against it, peering into the room. He is a strangely beautiful figure in evening dress, soft broad-brimmed hat and opera cloak. He wears a white mask, and white gloves. There is a hammering on the other side of the door from Raoul and the Phantom leans sharply towards the sound

After a moment, the hammering stops and Raoul backs slowly into the room

Locked! From the inside! ... but that's impossible, she...

Seeing the rose, he crosses quickly to it, kneeling. The Phantom leans to follow his movement. The music continues. Raoul lifts the rose to his nose, then — the hairs at the back of his neck rising — he suddenly turns to peer into the mirror — too late. The Phantom swings round and disappears upstage, the lighting reverting. If timed correctly, the mirror appears to shimmer, Raoul's reflection taking the place of the Phantom. Raoul stares into the mirror, leaning from side to side, almost sure he saw something. He faces front, then spins suddenly to take another look, hoping to take whatever it was by surprise, but there is still nothing there. He turns back front, his fury taking over

She *was* in here! ...Talking with a man! ... Unchaperoned in her dressing-room!

He sings

Song 3: How Dare She!

Raoul   How dare she!
                       Alone with a man!
                       Who is this creature?

This gross wretch
Who impertinently claims to love her?

*He rages about the room, looking for something to smash, but can only
weakly tip over Christine's chair*

My beloved, she is stolen!
And my rage a burning fury!
Tremble, villain!
And so, Christine, we are finished ...
Our love is over!
I say it's over...
Ended!

He hurls the rose to the floor and goes R. *Fast lighting change. The
Phantom runs to peer into the empty room through the mirror, then
turns to run back into the darkness. As he does so, the "Corridor" cloth
is lowered fast, the dressing-room door hinged off and Raoul reappears*
DR *to complete his song*

I've been provoked unbearably
Nothing can quench this fire in me
I hope he has a thousand lives
I'll commit as many murders
Is this how she repays me?
Alas, how she betrays me
She's all that's foul in womankind!
No!
No!
Ah!
No!
I must calm myself and cast her out of my life
Forget her
Forget her
Forget her
How dare she?
How dare she?
How dare she?!

He pauses, irresolute, unable to make up his mind whether to return to the dressing-room for a further search

He turns and strides off

As the music finishes, the Lights fade quickly to Black-out. All this is timed so that he disappears, the Lights snap out, and the play-off ends at the same time. After a moment, the cloth rises on:

SCENE 5

A Communication from the Ghost

Richard's office. A few days later

All is very bright and airy. There is a large window at the rear, Richard's keyhole desk UC, facing us with a chair behind. Two other chairs dress the scene UR and UL. Rémy is standing by the desk, R, sorting mail, as Richard enters quickly from L, now sporting a natty, light summer suit, little straw hat and carrying gloves and a cane, all of which he hands to Rémy after his entrance

Richard Morning, morning, morning, morning, morning, morning, morning!

Rémy Morning, sir.

Richard Don't interrupt, Rémy. Ever since the Coroner ruled "Accidental Death" last week, it's been one beautiful day after another. Isn't it amazing what a difference daylight makes? Everything's so — so —

Rémy (*carrying things off R*) Light, sir?

He exits

Richard (*partly following him*) For once, Rémy, you are right. Everything's light! Everything's luminous, lambent and lovely!

Madam Giry enters L carrying a letter

Richard turns

Well, nearly everything. What is it, Madam Giry?

Madam Giry I have a letter for you, sir.
Richard (*jovially, taking it from her*) What? The postman too, are we,
  Madam Giry? (*He crosses round to his desk* R)
Madam Giry I found it in Box Five.

Sting and segué underlay of the "Ghost" theme

The usual place.

Humming cheerfully, Richard sits to read

Richard Usual place? For what?

*He hums as he rapidly scans it, his jolly song clashing with ghostly
underlay. His expression alters, and he rises again, moving down the right
of the desk*

Good Heavens! Rémy! Come here and listen to this letter! It's — it's —

Rémy hurries back in

Rémy Bad news, sir?
Richard It's worse than that. Listen. (*He reads*) "Dear Mr Richard, I was
  most disappointed you saw fit to use my box on the night of the
  unfortunate Mephistopheles accident" ... His box, indeed! The scoun-
  drel! And look — the word "accident" has been underlined! ... "Please
  see that it doesn't happen again. Please also see that Christine Daaé
  sings the role of Marguerite when the production is resumed this
  evening. Do not fail me in this, or you must suffer the consequences.
  Your obedient servant, O.G."

The music stops and they stare at one another

Richard ⎫
Rémy ⎬ (*together*) O.G.?
Madam Giry Opera Ghost ...

Sting

— sir.

Richard So! The rogue's trying his vile tricks on me, is he? Well, not for very much longer. (*To Rémy as he bangs the letter down on the desk*) Send for Miss Daaé immediately!

Rémy (*putting his hand to the right of his chest*) Oh, may I, sir?

He hurries out L above Madam Giry

Richard I mean to get to the bottom of this, Madam Giry. (*He crosses R*) Nobody swindles this theatre while I'm in charge.

A commotion off L

Ah, here she is now. Come in, Miss Daaé.

The Groom enters quickly, crossing straight to Richard, snatching off his cap, followed by Rémy to LC

Groom Mr Richard! (*He emphasizes the "Rich"*)

Richard You're not Miss Daaé.

Groom Miss who?

Rémy I'm sorry, sir — this is the Groom.

Richard The what?

Rémy The Groom, sir.

Richard (*crossing to him*) Will you fetch Miss Daaé!

Rémy hurries out L

Groom Miss who?

Madam Giry (*to Richard*) He looks after the stables, sir.

Richard (*to Madam Giry*) What stables?

Groom The ones we keep the 'effin' 'orses in! Do me a favour, John! Are you Mutt and Jeff, or what? I mean, leave it out! You're gettin' on me West 'ams! Any more of this, and I'm leggin' it down the Frog and Toad back to 'Oxton! Strewth!

Brief pause

Richard (*to Madam Giry*) Why is he talking in this extraordinary way?

Madam Giry He's English, sir. We always have an Englishman to look after the horses. They get on so well together.

Richard What horses?

Groom The ones we keep in the stables! What's your game? Brain took a day off?

Richard would like to get his hands round the Groom's throat

Madam Giry You can't put an opera on with nothing but a load of music and singing, sir. The public won't stand for it. You've got to have hundreds of extras, thousands of costumes, acres of scenery, twenty-five minutes of ballet, and horses ... So we stable our own.

Richard And where precisely are these stables?

Groom Three cellars down, mate.

Richard Three? How many cellars are there?

Madam Giry Five.

Groom But we don't count the bottom one. Nobody goes down there. That's the one just over the lake.

Richard (*demented*) Lake? What lake?

Groom The underground lake this place was built on! How'd you get this job?

Richard would like to kill him

Madam Giry It's where the secret police dropped the bodies during the last uprising. There's a manhole in the floor of the bottom cellar, and the lake's full of bones. Now if you'll excuse me, I have to see to the ushers' soup.

She glides off L

Richard (*staring after her*) And I thought I was having trouble with Miss Daaé.

Groom Miss who?

Richard (*cracking and moving furiously up to his desk from the L*) Look, will you kindly come to the point, and tell me why you're here!

Groom (*keeping level with him R*) Well, all right! 'E's pinched one of the 'orses!

Richard 'Oo 'as? (*He collects himself*) Who has?

Groom The ghost has.

Clenching his fists in rage, Richard sinks down into his chair

Caesar, me best white stallion. *Aida*'s 'ad it.
Richard Listen! (*He bangs his fist on the desk*) You've got just one chance of prolonging your employment here! That is if you tell me the whole story! ... but in a manner befitting this noble establishment.
Groom (*shrugging*) If that's what you want, mate.

Music. He strides DR, and snaps a finger. Lights fade quickly and he is hit by a follow spot. As instructed by his superior, he sings opera

Song 4: Late Last Night I'm in the Cellars

Groom   Late last night I'm in the cellars ...
Black as pitch ... the gas is out ...
Old Mauclair, the lightin' fellow's
Fast asleep again, no doubt.
All at once there's this commotion
Caesar's restless and disturbed
Somethin's makin' 'im perturbed
And in spite of no light
I can see a weird sight
Clingin' on to Caesar's back
Dressed from 'ead to toe in black
Wiv a long flowin' cape
And a mask up to its forehead
Gallopin' 'im down the corridor
Is somethin' really 'orrid ...
Just a shape
Though I'm out of gas
I realize it 'as
To be ...
'Im
Am I gettin' through?
I'm one of very few
To see ...
'Im

Then I'm away, leggin' it like 'ell
Mister R, you should 'ave 'eard me yell
"Mauclair!"
"Are you there?"
"Where've you gone?"
"Anyone!"
"Everyone!"
"'Elp!"

He puts two fingers into his mouth and whistles piercingly, finishing in the same snapped-finger pose as he began, with the lighting restored immediately

Richard rises and comes round the desk from the L, deceptively calm

Richard A ghost?
Groom Right.
Richard On horseback?
Groom Correct.
Richard Galloping down the corridor?
Groom Got it.
Richard You're fired.
Groom (*crossing to him*) Do what, John?
Richard (*crossing to R, below him*) Get out, get out, get out!

Raoul enters from L, also dressed in a light summer suit, sweeping off his straw boater

Raoul Father, I must speak with you!
Richard Not now, Raoul.
Raoul But Father, my life is a shattered ruin!
Richard It can wait. (*To the Groom*) I thought I told you to —

Rémy enters L

Rémy Miss Daaé, sir.

Raoul moans and moves quickly up round the desk to the window, R

Groom Miss who?

Christine enters from L

Richard Will you go away!
Christine But you just sent for me, sir.
Richard Not you! (*To the Groom*) You!
Christine (*seeing him and moving up to the left corner of the desk*) Raoul!

Raoul moans again

Richard (*to Raoul*) Shut up! (*To the Groom*) Get out!
Groom I'm off, don't you worry about that. But you ain't firin' me. I come
in 'ere to get me cards, cos there's nothin'll get me down them cellars
again.

He speaks into Richard's face, making him flinch back R

   Nothin'!

He crosses L *and speaks into Christine's face, making her flinch upstage*

   Nothin'!

He goes L, *then returns to shout into Remy's face, causing him to flinch
back* L *and bang his head against the portal*

   Nothin'!

He finally exits L

Richard takes a deep breath, and begins again, crossing to Christine

Richard Now then, Miss Daaé, somebody is trying to make a monkey out
of me. Somebody is trying to pull the —
Rémy (*crossing right, holding his head*) Wool.

He goes, R

Richard (*glaring after him*) — over my eyes. Somebody is pretending to be a ghost. But I've seen through it. (*He crosses* DL) Oh yes, Miss Daaé. I believe this whole affair to be a put-up job — (*He crosses back to her* R) — a plot between you and your clique — (*He turns back to her*) — your *claque* — of friends — to see that you sing Marguerite in place of the great Carlotta again.

Rémy reappears, R, *with a glass of water, which Richard takes. Rémy exits*

Richard sits at the chair, R

What do you say to that?
Christine It's completely untrue, sir. (*She moves up a little, to Raoul*) Raoul, intercede for me. I don't understand you these past few days. You've been so cold, so cruel. Help me.

Brief pause

Raoul I'm afraid I can't.

He turns his back on her

Richard You see? Even my unfortunate son no longer takes your part. That will be all, Miss Daaé. Your contract is terminated. You will leave the Opera House immediately.

With a sob, Christine runs from the room L

Satisfied, Richard rises, crossing down to the portal, L. *The tortured Raoul moves down to the portal,* R

That is the end of that. As for Box Five, I shall use it whenever I please. It shall be my private box.

He leans against the portal, sipping his water. Raoul leans gloomily opposite

Ha! Ghosts, indeed! Some people will believe anything.

Scrape, and the "Ghost" music underlays all that follows. Lights check swiftly to a tight bright special on the desk, and two dimmer ones on Richard and Raoul. The Phantom's hand shoots up through a tiny hole in the top of the desk, bends to pick up the letter, crumples it, and takes it down out of sight

As for you, young man, I'm glad to see you've come to your senses, as far as this girl is concerned. You've obviously been seeing her behind my back.

During this and what follows, the hand produces another letter, takes the quill pen from the inkwell, signs the letter with a flourish

Raoul She loves another. I was thinking of going to the North Pole.
Richard Why?
Raoul It's never been done before.
Richard I see.

Scrape and the music stops, the hand sinking out of sight, the lighting reverting to normal. Raoul breaks from the portal, shaking off his mood

Raoul But tell me, Father, what's put you in such a foul temper? You were perfectly cheerful this morning.
Richard I will show you. (*He crosses to the desk and hands Raoul the letter*) Read that. (*He breaks back* DL)
Raoul (*not very interested*) "Dear Mr Richard, since you choose to defy me, I now give you a clear warning. (*His voice changes*) You must call back Miss Daaé immediately, and tell her she is to sing tonight, or—"
Richard That's not the letter! (*He snatches it from him and reads*) " — or suffer the consequences." (*He shouts*) Rémy! (*He resumes reading*) "You are also reminded that my allowance of 20,000 francs for the current month is still due. O.G."

Rémy hurries on from R *to peer over his shoulder*

(*To Rémy*) Did you put this letter on my desk?
Rémy No, sir.
Richard Then there's only one explanation! Miss Daaé must have slipped it there! Quickly, Rémy — after her!

He hurries off L, followed by Rémy

Raoul (*hurrying after them*) But, Father — Father!

Music. Fast fade to Black-out. The Corridor cloth flies in, Jammes takes her position, and the Lights build on:

SCENE 6

An Alternative Explanation

Outside Richard's office. Immediately following

The corridor is well-lit, but not too brightly. Jammes is on the floor R doing bone-cracking exercises with her foot round the back of her neck, etc. The men are heard off L approaching. There must be no delay here—Richard and Rémy continuing ad-lib from the office, entering L

Richard I tell you there is no other explanation! (*To Jammes*) You, girl! Where is Miss Daaé?
Jammes She's not here. She's gone. She went out. She's not here.
Richard Blast! (*He turns, crosses past Rémy to go L*)

Raoul enters L

Raoul Father, much as Christine has broken my heart, I'm sure she'd never deceive the management.
Richard You poor deluded boy, the girl is obviously a witch — an imposter.
Rémy (*quickly*) There may be another explanation, of course.
Richard Such as what?
Raoul (*crossing quickly to Rémy's right*) Yes, man, what?
Rémy Well ... the pressures of a great Opera House ... all sorts of unscrupulous people become involved. Beautiful and vulnerable creature that she is ... Heavens knows whose influence she may have come under.
Raoul Of course! Why didn't I think of it before?

He has turned to Jammes in his excitement, and she uses his hand as a bar

Somebody is manipulating her!

She uses his hand for support and pirouettes

Using her for his own ends! (*He passes her across him to his left*) Well,
he shan't succeed!

She poses low, one leg up, supported by him

He bends so that he can speak to her

Quickly, Jammes, where is she?
Jammes She's probably gone to the cemetery, sir.
Raoul The cemetery?
Jammes Yes. (*She breaks* R) You see, her father ... (*miming a beard*) ...
used to play the harp ... (*She mimes playing a harp on one knee*) ... in
the orchestra here ... (*she indicates it*) ... till he died ... (*grabbing her
heart and croaking*) ... and whenever she feels unhappy, she goes to
pray ... (*she mimes praying*) ... at his grave ... (*She finishes on a pose*)
and ask for advice.
Raoul The poor child! (*He crosses* L) I must go to her immediately.
Richard No, Raoul, come back!
Raoul Never, Father! Unless it be as her husband.

He goes, L

Richard The blind fool. His mother would turn in her grave if she hadn't
been lost at sea. (*To Rémy*) We will continue this investigation. (*He
crosses* L) Back —
Rémy (*following him*) To the office?
Richard I know where I'm going, Rémy. I'm not lost.
Rémy No, sir.

By now, they are offstage

Richard (*off*) Which way is it?

Music. Lighting checks. Jammes stretches

*Madam Giry glides on from R and takes her by the neck. Sting. Jammes
goes rigid*

Madam Giry You shouldn't have told them that. You'll have displeased
— him.

*She releases her. Jammes flies off L, darting quick glances back at Madam
Giry. Fade to Black-out with scene-change music. Segué introduction to
Song No. 5. The cloth rises slowly on:*

SCENE 7

The Angel of Music

A cemetery. Later

*A number of graves with one especially large one, its headstones facing
away from us, DC. Mist drifts. Christine, cloaked, enters UL, and makes her
way slowly through the headstones to a small one DR, where she kneels and
lays a small posy of white roses*

Christine Oh, Father, everything was going so well. But now ...

She sings
                    Song 5: All of my Dreams Faded Suddenly

All of my dreams faded suddenly
I felt our love was so sure
Being so sweet and heavenly
How could it fail to endure?
But then in one short moment
I find that I am alone

During the following, she wanders L

My life is over now
Soon I must go
Far from the memory
That haunts me so

How has it come to pass
This strange affair?
Whose is the shadow
That I feel is there?

*A shadow flits across her face and she darts upstage, looking about her.
Finding nothing, she wanders back DL, and then over to her father's grave
during the following*

Often I feel there is something in the night
Beating its dark wings above me
Filled with such envy and cruel spite
Hating whoever dares love me

My life is over now
Love passes by
Soon I must leave
I must say goodbye
Now that it's come to pass
What can I do?
There is no place for me
Here without you
All I have left is a broken vow
Truly my life is over now
My life is over now
Over now
My life is over now

Raoul (*off, speaking*) Christine!

He runs on UL

Christine!

*She turns. Both run to their right, in order to get round the big gravestone
between them. They stop and run to their left. Christine runs to her right
again, and Raoul holds up a hand, stopping her. He comes down the left-
hand side of the gravestone, and holds out his hands. They embrace*

Christine Oh Raoul, I thought I'd lost you forever.
Raoul I've been a fool, a selfish fool, I was — jealous.
Christine (*astounded*) Jealous? Of whom?
Raoul Of the person you sing for.
Christine (*frightened*) How do you know about that?
Raoul I followed you to your dressing-room after you ran off that night.
Christine (*turning away*) And?
Raoul I heard you sing to him.

She turns back quickly

> I didn't mean to eavesdrop, my darling. I simply have to know who it
> is.

Christine You may not believe me.
Raoul (*spreading his hands*) I ? Disbelieve *you* ?
Christine Then I will tell you. It was my Angel of Music.

*A long pause while Raoul looks at her, hands still spread, then he crosses
below her, to* R

Raoul Christine, you make fun of me. An Angel of Music?
Christine My father told me about him when I was little. There is an
Angel of Music in Heaven, he said — and when I die, I shall send him
down to teach you to sing. And it actually happened! My Angel of Music
came to me — and under his guidance, I've flowered, I've prospered.
Raoul But Christine, there is no such thing as an Angel of Music.
Christine (*going to him*) Oh, but there is, there is! Only he won't appear
while you're here. You must pretend to go away.

He protests

> Please, Raoul. For me.

Raoul (*melting*) Very well. (*He claps her on the arm, and speaks in a
gruff, hearty voice*) Well, Christine! It's getting late! Must dash! See
you in the morning! Cheeribye! (*He indicates below portal right,
whispering*) I'll be over here.

*He presses himself flat against the portal, right. Christine turns, the cloak
swirling, to lay a hand on the big gravestone, left, looking up*

Christine Come to me, my Angel of music ... Sing for me ...

A long pause. With a shrug, Raoul steps out, ready to chide her, but as he does so, there is a sound of thin, cold wind, of high strings, and he presses himself back. Shafts of light break through the clouds, striking down into the graveyard, transforming it into a place of great beauty, and the Angel (the Phantom) sings. During the song, Raoul moves slowly amongst the tombs looking about him, up into the shafts of light. Christine kneels, and he studies her rapt expression. Gradually, he too becomes still, hypnotised by the beauty of the song

Song 6: While Floating High Above

The Phantom   While floating high above
I hear you speak my name
Your voice so sweetly calling me
To come to you again
I stole into your dreams
I touched your soul to mine
I gave you music, and soon ...
You must rest here with me
Eternally

We'll share paradise
We'll share paradise

The music plays on below the dialogue that follows, but the Light slowly restores to normal. Raoul kneels beside Christine

Raoul Do you hear this at the Opera House too?
Christine (*still spellbound*) Coming from the very walls.
Raoul And he teaches you, talks to you?
Christine Yes.
Raoul In your dressing-room?
Christine Usually, yes.
Raoul Then, Christine, where were you?
Christine (*taken aback*) What do you mean?
Raoul After I heard you talking to your — Angel of Music — I went into

your dressing-room, but it was empty. There was nobody there. So where were you?

Christine (*rising, frightened*) I'm not sure.

Raoul (*rising with her*) But you must know! How could an Angel of your dreams spirit you away? And to where?

Christine I tell you I'm not sure! Oh, leave me alone!

She runs off UL, Raoul pursuing her

Raoul Christine! Come back!

But she has gone. The music finishes on a sinister note. An owl hoots, the Light dims, as Raoul moves back slowly downstage, his brain working very hard

An Angel of Music ... An Opera Ghost ... An Unexplained Death ... (*He has a brilliant thought*) Could these be related in some way? ... A child might believe in an Angel ... and a villain might take advantage of a child ... She may be in some danger. I'd better think.

He strikes various poses in an effort to do so, but it is obvious that thinking doesn't come easy to him. However, he is spared further embarrassment, for there is a sudden grating sound, echoing. Raoul becomes alert, clenches his fists, and looks from R to L downstage, backing up to the big headstone. The grating sound becomes a thin rustling. As Raoul hits the gravestone, he drops quickly to sit on a small ledge at its base. At the same time, there is a huge sting of music — enough to make everybody jump out of their seats — and the white-gloved hands of the Phantom shoot out from either side of the headstone. Raoul continues to peer alertly directly ahead, as they bend towards his throat. The music becomes thin and eerie. They make a sudden dart for him, but unfortunately the headstone is too wide, and they can't reach. They try again, still to no avail. They clench in frustration and disappear behind the headstone. The music changes again, as one hand now appears above the top of the headstone, holding a pebble, which it drops on Raoul's head, before disappearing again. Startled, Raoul looks directly up. Then he climbs up on the headstone to peer over. As he does so, the hands dart up and take him by the throat. The music becomes loud, dramatic as the dark shape of the Phantom rises up

*from behind the headstone, climbing to tower above Raoul as he throttles
him. He is a less distinct form this time, the mask black. Raoul's struggles
become weaker, and his arms fall to his sides. All seems over with him*

Gravedigger (*off*) Oy! What d'you two men think you're playing at?

The Phantom drops Raoul, runs DL, *jumps into the auditorium, and runs
to the rear as the Gravedigger enters* R, *carrying a spade and a lantern,
running across* DL *to call after the Phantom*

Oy! I'm talking to you! ... (*he turns back*) Cheeky devil. (*To Raoul*) Are
you all right, sir? Your face is all funny.
Raoul (*gasping*) Somebody just tried to kill me.
Gravedigger Well, he came to the right place.

*The sound of a galloping horse from the rear of the auditorium. Raoul
joins the Gravedigger in peering off at it, their heads close together*

Now look! He's riding a bloody great white horse clear across my
cemetery! (*With satisfaction*) Well he won't get out that way — he's
heading straight for the wall.

*Break in horses' hooves, their heads go up and down together, the hooves
pick up again, and fade*

Over the wall.
Raoul That horse will be Caesar, no doubt! (*He crosses up to right of the
headstone*) And yes, by thunder, look! This stone's been moved, and the
grave's empty! (*He calls off after the Phantom*) Angel of Music. (*He
bites his thumb at him*) I think not, my fine friend!

He hurries UL, *the Gravedigger following him round the gravestone to* UR

Gravedigger Just a minute —!
Raoul I haven't got a minute! I must return to the Opera House
immediately! ... God knows what's going on there!

As he runs off UL, *scene-change music, and Lights fade quickly to Black-
out. The Corridor cloth flies in. Lights build on:*

SCENE 8

A Vocal Problem

Outside Carlotta's dressing-room . A little later

*The corridor is brightly lit. Tuning-up noises are heard (from off stage—
not the pit), and the sounds of a violent argument. Carlotta strides on from
R, followed by Richard and — more slowly — Faust. She is in her
"peasant" costume but carries the same distinctive fan. Richard is in
evening dress. Faust is in his old man garb, but with the hood pushed back,
and a beard around his neck*

Carlotta No, no, no, I tell you I cannot continue! (*She tears off her blonde
plaited wig*) My nodules are swollen. (*Hoarse and tragic*) My voice has
gone. (*She screams off at the top of it*) Lisette!
Richard But you were doing splendidly. And there's a Persian out front.
He's come all the way from —
Faust Persia.
Carlotta Then I do not continue to croak in front of him.

*Lisette, her maid, runs on from L, with a spray. Carlotta opens her
mouth, indicates, and is sprayed*

Richard But, diva —
Carlotta (*her mouth open, telling him to go somewhere*) Uh ö.
Richard I'm sure we can solve this little problem, diva.
Carlotta You couldn't solve dividing four by two, you short-arsed little
frog. The Jewel Song is next — where the Devil tempts Marguerite with
a box of jewels — and I have to put them on while I sing. Have you any
idea how difficult that is? To sing and move at the same time? (*To
Lisette*) Order my carriage! I'll be in my dressing-room.

*Lisette flies off R as Carlotta moves to her dressing-room L, pursued by
Richard*

Richard But what about your next scene? We're just coming to your next
scene?
Carlotta (*off*) You can stick it up your —

A door slams

Faust Well, at least we've been spared the medical details.

He turns R and calls people to him. Music

> *Jammes, Lisette, Rémy and two Stagehands hurry on to see what's up, staying in a tight group R. The tuning-up noises stop. Faust sings to them:*

Song 7: She Says She's Got the Nodules

Faust   Carlotta ...
                        She says she's got the nodules
                        But not her ...
                        She's had a threat from 'him'
                        (*He indicates above*)
                        He told her
                        That if she went on singing
                        Her future
                        Could be rather grim

Carlotta bursts on from L, crossing past Richard, to C, wearing a turban and pulling on her wrap

Carlotta (*spoken to Faust*) And you keep your tubby torso out of this, you fat little faggot!
Faust (*spoken, furious*) What do you mean, *little*? (*He sings*)
                        I'm sick of all your prejudice
Carlotta   Then keep your big nose out of this!
Faust (*turning his back to her and lifting his robe*)
                        You know what you can come and kiss
Carlotta   It would be difficult to miss

She turns and Richard drops on his knees before her. Faust leans on the group, a suffering man

Richard   Please, diva, dear, on bended knee
                        I've cancelled one show recently

                             You really must go on for me
                             Or I'll become a mockery
Carlotta   You want me on the stage?
Richard   I do
Carlotta   Although my voice is dodgy?
Richard   True
Carlotta (*crossing him to* L)
                             All right, I do it, just for you
                             And you can do the singing, too!

She exits L

Richard (*rising*)   Me sing it?
The Rest (*looking front*)
                             That'll be the day (*They look back at him*)
Richard   Though someone should
The Rest (*looking front, mocking*)
                             Hip hip, hooray
Richard   But who, I wonder?

*Christine, still cloaked and carrying her music case is being ushered
past the group, from* R, *by Debienne*

                             (*Seeing Christine*) Miss Daaé!

She turns to run, but he grabs her

                             No, no, no, no, don't run away!
Christine   I'm sorry, sir, just passing through
                             I've come to clear my dressing roo —
Richard   And what a silly thing to do
                             How could we think of losing you
                             (*He leads her back to the group*)
                             Stand over there, keep still
Christine   Yes, sir
Richard (*crossing* L)
                             Keep very quiet
Christine   I will, yes, sir
The Rest (*looking off* R)
                             They're throwing things

Richard   Shut up!
The Rest (*looking at him*)
                        Yes, sir
Richard   Now watch me make it up to her.
                        (*He raps the portal*) Oh diva, dear ...
Carlotta (*off*)   Drop dead
Richard   It's me.
Carlotta (*off*)   I do not leave this room
Faust (*crossing to* c)Whoopee!

A screaming Carlotta reappears, making for him

Carlotta   Ah ...!

He scoots to the back of the group. She turns to go back into her room, but Richard is in the way

Richard   I've got a plan which I submit
                        You mime the scene and (*he demonstrates*) gesture
                           it
                        (*He crosses to Christine*)
                        Miss Daaé does the singing bit
                        We'll ...shove her in the pit
Christine (*moving forward*)
                        Oh, really, Mr Richard —
Richard   What?
Christine   I —
Richard   Want your job back?
Christine   Like a shot
Richard (*leading her back to the group*)
                        Then shut up while I butter up
                        Our diva
Debienne (*pulling her into the group*)
                        Get the plot?

Richard turns to Carlotta, all over her, speaking a language she understands

Richard   Your audience awaits

> Their favourite scene of yours
> So famous for "The Jewel Song"
> Which always creates
> Tumultuous applause
> Because your acting is so strong
> (*He crosses to* L)
> She sings your famous aria
> They think it's you, *et cetera*
> Your public yell and shout huzza
> The biggest thing in opera

The music stops. The group lean in as Carlotta considers

Carlotta (*speaking to Richard, her fan masking them from Christine*)

> Well ... she sounds like a toad. But ...
> (*She sings*) If I sing Juliet in
> That new opera by Gounod

Seeing himself as the obvious candidate for the other role, Faust steps out of the group to strike a pose. The group lean back, and Carlotta points at Faust without looking at him

> And this decrepit cretin
> Isn't Romeo

Faust reacts

Richard   Do you know ...
               I think I might agree
Carlotta   It's a deal?
Richard   Cross my heart
Carlotta   Then tell 'em all from me
               That I'm prepared to start

During the final three lines, the Stagehands and Lisette exit R

The remainder form a line, Rémy to R, *then Jammes, Faust, Christine, Richard, Carlotta and Debienne*

All   She is prepared to start
                       She's quite prepared to start
                       The star, the star's prepared to start

*All pose. During the applause, Richard breaks the line, leading Carlotta
back to her dressing-room*

Richard Diva, diva, you have saved the day! A million gratitudes! (*He
shouts off as the applause ends*) Get her back into her costume! (*To the
others*) Places, everybody!

All hurry off R

Richard follows them, leading Christine by the hand

I'm sorry I shouted at you earlier. It's because I like you. We'll be
starting with the Jewel Song, if you want to check anything.

He shoves her off R

Somebody get her in the pit! And send Madam Giry to me immediately.
(*He crosses* L *at the same time as Faust crosses* R, *creating a "scissors"*)
No so-called ghost gets the better of me.
Faust Ha!
Richard Oh, Claude. We'll think of another role for you instead of
Romeo. (*He crosses further,* L) What's that other opera? Pagli —
pagli—
Faust (*eagerly*) — acci!
Richard Right!

He exits L

Overcome with emotion, Faust strikes a pose and sings

Faust   Ridi, paggliacco
                       Sul tuo amore infranto!

Madam Giry enters from L

Now he even has someone to sing to. He switches the remainder of the aria to her, crossing to R *before the end, singing very closely and intimately, a catch in his throat*

> Ridi del duol
> Che t'avvelena il cor

Madam Giry Bugger off.

Faust takes out a big white handkerchief, and goes, R, *mopping his brow, shocked*

Richard reappears from L. *Tuning-up noises are heard from off*

Richard Ah, there you are, Madam Giry. I shall watch the remainder of the performance from my usual box, if you don't mind — Box Five — and La Carlotta shall continue in the role of Marguerite ...

He goes DR, *jauntily. Tuning-up noises stop, and sombre music from the orchestra takes over. The lighting checks*

Madam Giry He'll soon find out who sings like a toad around here. (*She crosses slowly* L) I keep warning them. Don't provoke *him*, I say. But does anybody listen? They do not. (*As she goes,* L) God knows what'll happen tonight. God knows.

Light fade quickly to Black-out. Segué drum roll into live tuning-up noises in the pit. In the Black-out, the curtains fly in, closed, the boxes truck on. Light builds on:

Scene 9

A Farewell Performance

The stage and auditorium. Immediately following

The Persian enters Box Six. He is a tall, dark, sinister figure in a black coat, astrakhan collar and hat. He stands. Richard almost falls into Box Five. He shows the conductor two crossed fingers, then sees the Persian. They look hard at one another, sitting slowly, not taking their eyes off one another. Raoul hurries into Box Five — having changed into evening dress

Raoul Father, I think we should hold the curtain! I have some vital new information concerning the ghost!

Richard Don't be ridiculous.

Raoul But Father, something terrible's happened!

Richard And something terrible's going to happen on stage, if this goes wrong.

Raoul sees Debienne in the auditorium, helping Christine clamber into the orchestra pit, whispering

Raoul What's Christine doing?

Richard What does it look like she's doing? She's singing the Jewel Song for us.

Music begins, and Lights start to fade

Raoul But surely Carlotta's doing Marguerite tonight?

Richard Carlotta is miming the role — (*he demonstrates with his fingers*) — your girlfriend is going to sing it for her down there. Now shut up!

The curtain rises on a room in a large house, since that is the way the scene is being produced this year. To the rear, the usual Faust *cloth*

R *and* L, *two chairs. Flown above* C, *a large, heavy-looking iron candelabra on chains, all very medieval.* DC, *the large, ornate jewel box*

Carlotta enters, and tumultuous applause greets her

She basks in it then calms it down, indicating her throat: she is about to sing. She points dramatically backwards to the jewel box without looking at it

Song 8: What Do I See?

Carlotta/Christine What do I see?

She trips UL

From whence comes this most wondrous ornate casket?

She trips further, singing an aside to Richard

> I scarely dare touch it
> But why not?

She points

> I see the key to it

She picks it up

> Dare I unlock it?
> My hand trembles

She makes her hand tremble, looking at it. Unfortunately, Christine sings on here

> But why?

Carlotta faces front and mimes, "But why?". But it is too late

> I'll do no harmful wrong if I only peep inside it.

She kneels, shoves in the key, gives it two big twirls, flings open the lid, and sways back in astonishment

> What joy!
> It's full of wealth!

She takes out a glittering necklace

> Are they real (*she bites one*) or is this a charming
>   dream?
> I feel I'm swooning

She swoons on the floor, but gets up again quickly

> Mine eyes have never seen such a treasure of jewels!

One after another, she piles five necklaces around her neck, brings out a hand mirror, trilling

Ah ...

She trots DR *and stares in rapture at the mirror*

The joy!
I am now so beautiful to see

She pirouettes

Ah, the joy!
I am now so beautiful to see

Carlotta crosses L, *to lean on Richard's box, ogling him*

Is it you?
Marguerite?
Is it you?
Answer, do
Answer, do
Mirror, mirror, tell me quickly

She runs in a semi-circle round the stage, jumping over the jewel box, trilling

Ah—

But this time, the trill ends in the hideous croak of a toad. All those in the boxes react forward in astonishment. She tries again, and there is another croak. She makes one final determined effort. And this time she croaks twice. Richard hurriedly leaves the box and Raoul leaps into the pit

Carlotta (*to the conductor*) Stop it, stop it, you unutterable fool! (*She looks for Christine, who seems to have sunk down out of sight*) Don't let her out of the pit! I'm going to kill her!
M.D. I think she's fainted.

By now Raoul is supporting Christine

Richard, Rémy, Debienne, Madam Giry and Jammes run onstage, Jammes clearing the jewel-box

Raoul Christine!
Richard What's happened to her?
Raoul (*supporting her*) She appears to be drugged, Father.
Richard Then who was making those extraordinary noises?

The booming, echoing laugh of the Phantom rings around the auditorium, and the chandelier glows with bright light. All stare out front

The Phantom (*off*) She was singing to bring down the chandelier.
Richard The chandelier!

The sound of hacksawing and tinkling of crystal, and the chandelier above the audience begins to swing alarmingly. All rush to the front, and in ad-lib try to persuade the audience of their danger, and get them to move

Carlotta stays UC

All this should be allowed to continue as long as possible before being interrupted

The Phantom (*off*) No!

All stop. The hacksawing stops

Not *that* one! (*His voice becomes honeyed, intimate and moves to the stage*) *This* one.

With a gasp, all turn to look. Carlotta stares at them, then up at the iron candelabra above her head. She screams. All Lights snap off except for two tiny specials, angled upwards to light only the candelabra. It drops out of the light, fast. There is a instantaneous Black-out using black-out cards — and an almighty and lengthy crash. A pause, then the lighting is restored. Carlotta lies under the ruined candelabra in a pall of smoke and dust. All gasp and hurry up to surround her — all except Faust who only strolls UL, *examining his fingernails*

Faust Well. That's cured her nodules.

All stare at him. Black-out. Music. The curtains fly fully out, the Corridor cloth comes in, the boxes truck off, and Light builds on:

SCENE 10

The Ghost's Allowance

A corridor near the stage. Later the same night

The scene is not too brightly lit. The weary Richard trudges on from R, *followed by Rémy*

Richard All I want is one nice normal performance. Is that too much to ask?

Rémy Not really, sir.

Richard And all because of a fallacious Phantom whose alleged existence is being perpetuated by some trickster who wants a free box every night, and his girlfriend singing Marguerite. Well, he's not going to make me do it, Rémy. Because he doesn't frighten me — nothing frightens me.

Madam Giry, carrying another letter, makes a silent entrance from L

Richard turns L *to find Madam Giry. He nearly has a heart attack*

What is it *now*, Madam Giry?

Madam Giry I have another letter for you, sir — from him.

Richard (*snatching it*) How dare him! (*He rips it open*) Heads are going to roll for this, Madam Giry, and yours could well be the first!

The 'Ghost' music underlays as he reads

'Dear Mr Richard, the shock of poor Carlotta's accident' —underlined again, you see —' has reminded me that you have not yet paid me my allowance of 20,000 francs for this month. Accordingly, I have instructed Madam Giry to follow a different procedure on this occasion. Yours faithfully, O.G.' ... You see? Allowance, indeed! Well, this time the thief's gone too far, because this time we shall catch him! (*He gives the letter to Rémy, then turning to Madam Giry, he becomes excessively charming*) Would you mind awfully telling me what is this 'different procedure', Madam Giry?

Madam Giry I don't see why not. Acting under our Ghost's instructions, I extracted 20,000 francs from this month's income from the boxes, which I then gave to Mr Rémy.

Rémy You did *what?*

Madam Giry (*to Richard*) Those, sir, were my instructions — to slip the money into Mr Rémy's pocket when he wasn't looking. Needless to say, I did it easily.

A pause as Richard slowly turns to Rémy

Richard (*quiet and deadly*) So, Rémy. Et tu, Judas? Mine own faithful servant, a worm in the apple ... (*He grabs him in an armlock, and sticks his hand in Rémy's pocket*) Is this the pocket, Madam Giry?

Madam Giry Yes, sir.

Richard Empty! (*He releases him*) Well, Rémy? What have you got to say for yourself?

Rémy (*rubbing his arm*) I swear I know nothing about it, sir.

Richard You must! Otherwise, how was the money spirited from you pocket?

Rémy (*fed up*) Well perhaps there *is* a Ghost.

Richard (*beside himself*) I am sick and tired of saying there are no such things! ... (*with enormous irony*)... unless, of course, some 'Ghost' wafted it out of your pocket and put it into —

He breaks off, his hand in his pocket

Madam Giry Something the matter, sir?

He brings out a piece of paper and reads it

Richard 'Received with thanks the sum of 20,000 francs, O.G.' (*Brokenly*) O.G. ...

Music — slightly comic. He moves slowly to R, a beaten and a broken man

Rémy (*smugly*) Is there anything we can do, sir?

Richard Mm? Oh, no, no Rémy, just — just —

Rémy Carry on, sir?

Richard Yes, that'll be fine ... Oh, and you'd better put Miss Daaé's name
   in the —
Rémy Programme?
Richard She'll be singing Marguerite tomorrow.

   Richard exits

   *The music becomes sinister, the lighting checks, Madam Giry glides up
   behind Rémy*

Madam Giry It always gets them like that the first time——

Rémy jumps

   —when they discover 'he' really does exist.

She goes L. *He stares after her, then up at the gathering gloom. As he goes
to run, off* R, *fade to Black-out. The music builds into a crescendo of cymbal
roll, and the cloth rises on:*

SCENE 11

The Phantom of the Opera

The roof. A little later

At the rear, facing away from us, is the huge statue of Apollo. To the R *and
the* L *of it, filling the second portal, are balustrades. Similar balustrade
pieces run* DR *and* DL, *angled so as to permit an entrance between them and
the first portal. The sky is full of stars, and a thin wind blows. Wearing a
shawl, Christine stands to* L *of the statue, staring out at the night sky. An
old man enters* R, *strewing bird-seed*

Old Man Here, birdies ... Here, birdies ... (*He sees her*) Hallo, miss.
Christine Hallo.
Old Man What are you doing on the roof this time of night?
Christine I might ask you the same.
Old Man Oh, I've worked here for years — they let me do as I please now
   — (*crossing* L) — but I shouldn't stay too long — it gets a bit nippy this

high up. (*He strews some seed*) Here, birdies ... here — (*He swallows a handful, his mouth full*) — birdies ...

He goes, L. *There is a pause*

The Phantom (*off, very faint*) Chris — tine ...

She reacts, turning front, DL, *frightened*

Raoul (*off, faint*) Christine...!

She reacts in relief, believing it to have been Raoul she heard the first time. He hurries on from R

Christine! (*He goes to her*) What are you doing up here? (*He takes her hand and leads her* R) Come back down.

Christine (*resisting*) No.

Sting, and music underlays all that follows. She pulls him back to C

Everything down there belongs to *him*. I know that now. I've known it ever since you spoke to me in the graveyard. Until then, I thought it was only a dream.
Raoul I don't understand.
Christine Listen, and I'll tell you. (*She crosses* R) It was the night Mephistopheles was killed — the night you came to my dressing-room.
Raoul When I heard you talking to — your Angel of Music?
Christine Yes, he came to comfort me — or so I thought — it had all been so awful. And then, a strange thing happened — something I'd never seen before. (*She crosses* L) The mirror began to spin ... faster and faster ... and all of a sudden, I was on the other side ... I was there.
Raoul Where, Christine?
Christine I don't know. It was almost black. But Caesar was there, too — the white horse that vanished ... And standing beside him ——this mysterious figure.

The music changes as the white-gloved hand of the Phantom appears from behind the statue. During the following, the Phantom slowly edges round, reacting to all he hears until he towers above them

Raoul What did he look like?
Christine I couldn't tell. He wore a mask. You must understand I thought I was dreaming. How was it possible unless it were a dream?
Raoul You must tell me, Christine. It's perfectly safe. We're quite alone. Tell me about your dream.
Christine He put me up onto Caesar's back, and led me down ... down through corridors and strange traps ... (*She crosses* R) Sometimes, in the distance, I could see men working at boilers or gas lamps, but they never seemed to see us ... We went down, further down — until we came to a lake ... (*She turns to him*) Raoul, there *is* a lake below the Opera House! There's an island on it, and that's where he lives.
Raoul Forgive me, Christine, but I can't ...
Christine (*going to him*) It's true! Believe me! He wanted me to stay there with him forever.
Raoul The swine.
Christine No, Raoul, he loves me. Oh, how he loves me. It breaks my heart.
Raoul (*hurt*) Christine ...

He turns away, and she moves quickly round to his left

Christine Oh no, Raoul, I told him I couldn't stay. And he did let me go ... but only after I promised to sing Marguerite one last time. And then I seemed to wake up in my dressing-room, as if from a dream. It was only when you told me that you had found it empty that I began to suspect. And when I heard his voice and the chandelier fell, I knew. It was no dream, and there was no Angel of Music. The man was real. And who else could he be but the one we call ... the Phantom of the Opera?

The music stops. He takes her hands

Raoul Christine, I'm going to take you away from all this danger.
Christine No, I must keep my promise. Mr Richard has asked me to sing Marguerite tomorrow, and I must.
Raoul Then after the performance? Will you come away with me then?
Christine Yes, it's for the best. (*She sinks to the floor*) Poor Phantom. Poor little ghost.
Raoul (*kneeling beside her*) How can you pity the creature? The man's mad.

Christine Mad with love. And yet I can't return it, all of my love is for you.

A faint sigh from the Phantom

(*Startled*) What was that?

Music. The Phantom presses himself to the right side of the statue as Raoul looks around

Raoul Just the wind. (*He holds her*) It's all right, we're quite alone.

The music continues as the Phantom returns to tower above them. The music builds to a crescendo, and he lifts his arms. It seems he must leap down on them, but he sags and the music quietens

The Phantom (*faint, tortured whisper*) Oh, Christine... You... betray... me ...

He sings

Song 9: To Pain My Heart Selfishly Dooms Me

The Phantom	To pain my heart selfishly dooms me My senses have devoured my soul This cruel love tortures, consumes me Love I know I will never control
Raoul	Mad with passion, I bow before you Till the day hell makes you my bride I despise and I adore you I only want to die by your side Full of joy, how I adore you With a love I cannot hide Oh, Christine, how I adore you Soon heaven will make you my bride
The Phantom	My dreams delude me Devouring my soul I curse this love that so eludes me

This love I cannot seem to control
I despise and adore you
My heart so lost before you
I despise and I adore you
How I wish that I controlled my feeble soul
I try to turn away
But know that I adore you
You will always be mine
Be mine

Raoul Take my heart
The willing heart you stole
I am yours
Your love subdues me
Oh, Christine, how I adore you
Must I say how I adore you
Must I say how I'll always adore you?
Every glance confesses my longing
Every sigh is so revealing
They show I'm under your spell
They show that I adore you
You'll always be mine
Be mine

Christine This man has conquered and wooed me
I have lost my heart and soul
I am yours
Love has subdued me
And it's a love I cannot control
My own one, I adore you
Surrendering unto your charms
I softly fell into your arms
I give all my love, I give all my love to you
I give all my heart, I give my heart to you
My own one, I adore you, my own one, I adore you
You'll always be here in my heart, my heart
So be mine

Play-off begins as Raoul helps her to her feet

Raoul Come. My coach will be at the rear of the building immediately after the performance tomorrow and then we shall be gone — far away from this devilish place.

He leads her off, R. The music changes as the Phantom jumps from the statue. It seems he must chase after them and tear Raoul apart, but he cannot. He rages, then slumps, defeated

Old Man (*off*) Here, birdies ...

The music changes as the Phantom tries to hide behind the statue R

The Old Man enters L, strewing some seed

Here birdies ... (*He sees the Phantom*) Hallo, who are you?

The music builds, the rage and grief explodes. The Phantom takes him by the throat

No! No!

The Phantom forces him off R

The Phantom reappears, to drag him across stage, L. The Old Man has been swapped for a dummy, but the actor still speaks the dialogue. The Phantom lifts him high

No! No! Put me down!

The music stops as the Phantom hurls him over the balustrade, L, into the night, his long, dying scream echoing as it fades. Timpani roll, and the Phantom runs DC, where the Lights pick him out

The Phantom (*screaming*) Christine! ... You will be mine!

He turns to move upstage. Music, to a finish, the Lights fading to Blackout. The curtain flies in, the boxes truck on, the House Lights and Chandelier build to full

CURTAIN

ACT II

SCENE 1

A Master Stroke

The stage and auditorium. The following evening

Dim house Lights to half. Entr' acte. House Lights down. Segué tuning-up noises from the band. Lights build on the curtains and boxes. After a moment, Richard enters Box Six. He glares at Box Five, then slumps, defeated. Raoul appears, gesturing urgently offstage, checking his watch, backing into Richard

Richard Oh, do sit down! Nothing's going to happen now the blasted girl's singing. It's what the Ghost wants, isn't it?
Raoul (*sitting*) So that's why we're in this box. You believe in him now.
Richard I didn't say that.

The tuning-up noises stop, and the Persian enters Box Five in the silence. He doesn't sit, but looks carefully about the auditorium

Richard and Raoul react, leaning forward

Raoul I say! Who's that sinister-looking fellow?
Richard Some Persian prince. He was here the night Carlotta got chandeliered. He's insisted on coming again. He must want to see *Faust* pretty badly, that's all I can say.

Music, and the Lights begin to dim

Oh, good. Only the last bit to go.
Raoul Yes, we're in for a treat now. This is where the *rejuvenated* Faust appears.

The curtains open on a dimly lit scene. The usual Faust *cloth at the rear, a low palliasse to the* R *on which reclines Christine, dressed in a pretty white shift, her hair down*

Song 10: Ah! Do I Hear My Lover's Voice?

Faust (*off*)   Marguerite!

Christine sits up, and a follow spot picks her out

(*Off*)Marguerite!

Christine   Ah! Do I hear my lover's voice?
                                        That dulcet sound from days gone by?

Faust springs on from L, *to strike a manly pose in a follow spot. He has been forced into a doublet many sizes too small, wears a rather striking cod-piece, and long golden locks cascade on his shoulders, surrounding a rouged and powdered face*

Faust   Marguerite!
Christine   Louder than the laugh of the demons
                                        Delighting in my ruin
                                        His voice rings out above
Faust (*moving a little towards her, holding out his hand, but still facing front, his teeth gleaming*)
                                        Marguerite!
Christine   His hand, his hand is here to save me!

At least, it would be if Faust wasn't so busy playing front that he doesn't notice that she can't reach it

He approaches

She stretches for the hand, and he takes it upon himself to move DL *at this point. She falls off the palliasse*

He has come!

She manages to get up

I am free
Behold my brave incomparable love

She moves to him. He strikes a pose, turned away from her, his left hand held high

Ah! 'tis thou, my dear one
Thou, 'tis thou, my dear one

During this, Faust becomes aware that the ring on his left hand doesn't gleam as it should, and he breathes on it, polishing it on his shirt

Nor death nor damnation
Can make my heart afraid

He crosses her to R, to strike another pose. She follows to C. It should be noted that although Christine is bewildered that he doesn't appear to be following the directions she was given, she is too inexperienced, the evening too thrilling an affair, for her to think of fighting back

Now love, we are one
Darkness overcome

Faust wriggles uncomfortably. His tights are creased underneath somewhere, and he has to ease them

Love and joy abound
Love and joy abound

He clears his throat, tosses his curls, his expression becoming glazed as he counts himself in

As oft in hope I prayed

Coming in incorrectly, Faust strides to C to sing, totally masking Christine who finds herself standing immediately behind him

Faust   Yes, 'tis I, my dear one
Satan's darts, I fear none

Timidly, Christine moves R, *and Faust chooses exactly the same time to move* R *himself, shaking his fist at the demons, masking her again*

> A curse on the demons
> Who so torment your soul

He takes her by the hand, leads her to the palliasse and throws himself down on it

> Safe now that I've found thee

Christine (*pulled to her knees*)
> Safe now

Faust (*pulling her round so that she faces his stomach*)
> My arms will be round thee

He drops her, rises, moves back to C. *Richard restrains Raoul*

Christine   Thy arms

She rises, goes to him

Faust   }
Christine   }   (*together*) Then we'll go to heaven

She gets into his arms, L

Faust   }   (*together*) We'll go up to heaven
Christine   }   My love, come, come, to my arms

As they hit their top notes, snap to Black-out. A scream. Commotion from Box Six, Lights revert. Faust is still holding his note, but his arms are empty

Raoul (*jumping out of the box*) She's gone! Where's she gone?

He runs off, L

Faust (*singing perfectly in time*)
            Marguerite!
Richard (*completely fed-up*) Oh, shut up!

He leaves the box. The puzzled Faust looks at his empty arms, around him, under him

A Voice, pretending to be an irate member of the audience, comes from rear of auditorium

Voice Right, that's it! I'm not coming here again! This bloody Opera never gets finished!

Raoul runs back on

Raoul (*to Faust*) What happened to her?
Faust I didn't notice, I was singing.

He exits R

Raoul She's completely disappeared!

Timpani roll. The Lights flicker a few times, then almost go out, just a dim downlight on Raoul

  Oh, my God! Of course! *Him*! (*He hurls orders off*) Get lanterns, everybody! Clear the auditorium! She must be found! It's a matter of life and death!

He runs off

The curtains fall into place, and people appear in the auditorium, with lanterns, Debienne down aisle R, Stage Hands and Lisette extreme R and L, and along the front, if there is room. Dominique, an usher, is in the dress circle, if there is one. There is only a glimmer of light. Each lights his own face by holding the lantern close to it

Richard (*appearing in the curtain split, carrying his lantern*) There's no sign of her backstage. (*He calls out front*) What about my staff? Any sign out there?

Song 11: No Sign! I See No Sign!

Debienne   No sign! I see no sign!
Richard   Where's that?
Debienne   I'm in row nine

Raoul enters through the curtain split, with his lantern, crossing down R

Raoul (*speaking*) Christine!

Rémy follows him carrying his lantern, going DL *and out into the auditorium to work in the aisle,* L

Rémy   She can't have vanished into air!
Richard (*speaking*) Circle!
Domique   There's no-one here
Richard   You're sure?
Domique   I swear
Richard (*speaking*) Gallery!

Faust has appeared here, with his lantern, by now

Faust   We've had a look around
The Rest   And?
Faust   Not a sign
Raoul   Search on, she must be found
Domique (*speaking*) Dress circle clear!
Richard   Light! We need light!
                 Where is Mauclair tonight?
Rémy (*speaking*) He can't be found, either! He's vanished, too
Richard   He's fired, if it's true
Raoul   I'm certain she's here
                 Concealed in this gloom
                 You go that way, you go there
                 I'll try her room

He goes back through the split

Faust (*speaking*) There's no sign up here!

Debienne (*speaking*) Or here!
Rémy (*speaking*) Or here!
Richard   Well, what about the bar?
Debienne (*speaking*) We've already searched it!
Richard   Then search again!
Faust   I've had a thought instead
                      Let's all go home and go to bed

*Jammes hurries through the split, carrying a tiny table, her long black
hair fallen out of her bun, picked out in a soft follow spot*

Jammes (*speaking;excited*) It's all right! Madam Giry knows how to find
Christine! She's going to read the tea-leaves! (*She moves* R *and poses*)

Richard (*in a madhouse again*)
                      Read the *tea-leaves* ?

*Like a high priestess, Madam Giry appears through the split, carrying
a tray of tea-things, in a follow spot. Richard is on stage,* L. *The others
hurry to form groups on the steps* R *and* L, *the only important position
being that Faust should be* R

Madam Giry (*waving her hands over the pot*)
                      Demon of tea, I conjure thee!
                      Appear in this infusion!
                      (*She pours*) Brewed in a pot and poured in a cup
                      We'll see what your tea-leaves tell

*She jerks her head at her acolyte and Jammes hurries across to Richard
to propel him a little towards Madam Giry, who advances on him, holding
out the cup*

                      Come drink the dark-brown mystic brew
                      But leave all the dregs behind

*Jammes hinges Richard's elbow forward and Madam Giry places the cup
in his hand, then crosses* R, *below the table*

                      Me, I'll decipher the shape that they make
                      By use of my expert mind

Jammes pushes Richard a little downstage and Madam Giry, with finger pointed, advances on him

> Go on and take a lovely slurp
> And if I'm any judge
> (*She pushes the cup to his lips*)
> The bits at the bottom will point to Christine...

She snatches the cup and saucer from him

> Don't swallow the tea-leaves, you twerp!

She crosses back R, upending the cup into the saucer, followed by Jammes, who gives Richard a pitying look

> And now to probe this wet mysterious sludge

She bends low, R handing the cup backwards to Jammes, who strikes a pretty pose

Faust (*tapping his head significantly*)
> I don't believe her

All except Madam Giry and Jammes She's got to be joking
> She's losing her marbles
> We'll have to send for the men in the white coats

Madam Giry (*excited*)
> Look here!
> See here!
> A clue revealed!

Faust (*hurrying to her*)
> What does it say?

Madam Giry   A tall dark stranger will come into your life

Although Faust likes the sound of this, the rest are fed up

All except Madam Giry
> But what about Christine?
> What about her?

Madam Giry (*peering out front, feeling the vibrations*)
>   She's near us
>   Very near us

Fast tempo. All scurry across the stage and out into the auditorium, except Richard, Jammes and Madam Giry. In the scurry, Jammes quickly clears the props through the split, then moves down R. *Richard goes* L, *Madam Giry* C. *The rest sing in the auditorium, using every available space*

All   Miss Daaé!
                       Can you hear us call?
                       It's us!
                       It's us!
                       Your friends
                       Miss Daaé!
                       Can you hear us call?
                       Miss Daaé!
                       It's us!
                       Your friends
                       It's us!
                       Your friends
                       It's us!
                       Your friends

Richard goes through the curtains, L, *Jammes through the curtains,* R, *Madam Giry through the curtains,* C, *the remainder using all available exits, timing to leave just as they finish singing. The last thing we see is Madam Giry, who turns sharply front as the music finishes. Snap out the follow spot, together with snap to Black-out. Segué scene change music. The boxes truck off, and the curtain rises on:*

SCENE 2

The Entrance to the Underworld

Christine's dressing-room. Immediately following

The room as before, but lit a little brighter. Raoul hurries in from R, *carrying his lantern, halting* LC, *puzzled to find the room still lit. There is*

*a ripple of Eastern music, and the Persian peels himself from off the hat
stand, R, where he has been concealed, like a suit of clothes. Raoul
becomes aware of the presence behind him, and turns sharply, reacting
back*

Raoul What are you doing here?
The Persian You are not going to find her like this, my young friend.
Raoul What do you know about all this?
The Persian Enough that we may yet save her.

*He points a pistol at Raoul, who gasps and raises his hands. But the
Persian reverses it and hands it to him*

Here. Take this pistol.

Raoul puts the lantern on the dressing-table, glancing at the pistol

Raoul It's not loaded.
The Persian Bullets are useless against him. To protect yourself, you
must always hold it so. (*He produces his own pistol and jumps into a
position, legs straddled, the barrel held up vertically against his nose*)
Ha!
Raoul Really, sir.
The Persian If you wish to rescue the young lady, and survive this night,
you must attend me. Ha! (*He jumps into the position again*)

The force of his personality forces Raoul to immediately follow suit

Raoul Ha!
The Persian (*examining him critically*) Very good. (*He puts his gun away
and moves up to the potted plant*) Whenever danger threatens, keep it
like that — always.
Richard (*off*) Putting the dressing-rooms at the top of the theatre! I've
never climbed so many steps.

*He runs in from R, followed by Rémy, both still carrying lanterns, across
to Raoul, who automatically drops into the position*

Raoul Ha!

Richard (*skidding to a halt*) Raoul, what are you doing?
The Persian (*moving* DR) He is obeying my instructions, Mr Richard.

Richard and Rémy turn to him

Richard Good heavens! It's the Persian Prince.
The Persian I have many titles. The Shah of the Oasis. The Sultan of
  Samarkand. But I am best known as the Great Mysterioso — (*He plucks
  a cigarette out of the air*) — Conjurer to Kings — (*He takes a lighted
  match from his lapel and holds it to the cigarette*)
Richard Why, you — you —
Rémy Imposter!
Richard Thank you, Rémy.

Pleased, Rémy crosses up and looks under the dressing-table

The Persian Forgive the deception, but it was necessary to gain
  admittance here undetected.

*He crosses R and examines the moulding on the portal. Seeing him do this,
Raoul does the same, L*

Richard And just how, sir, are you involved in Miss Daaé's disappearance?
The Persian In no way, my friend. I could never have spirited her away
  so adroitly, and there is only one better than myself — *him*.
Richard You don't mean — *him* him?

*Behind them, Rémy leans against the mirror and it spins on its central axis,
edge on to the audience, revealing blackness beyond. Music*

The Persian I do.
Rémy Good heavens, sir, look at this!
Richard Quiet, Rémy.
Rémy But, sir—!
Richard Not now, Rémy! I'm thinking.

*Richard moves R, above the Persian, almost off stage, thinking. The
Persian and Raoul are examining their mouldings, R and L. Rémy shrugs,
lifts the lantern, and goes behind the mirror. A timpani roll, and the mirror*

*closes on him. We see him through the mirror turn and tug at it, unable to
open it. He waves at them—at first easily, then more frantically, his mouth
opening and shutting, but no sound being heard*

*The Phantom appears behind him, puts a white-gloved hand over his
mouth, and drags him off into the darkness. Rattle from the band*

Richard (*moving back onstage*) All right, I've thought.
Raoul Yes?
The Persian And?
Richard What the hell's going on? And what exactly is your connection
with this 'him' fellow?
The Persian (*crossing to the dressing table*) Let us only say the man you
call the Phantom once spent a great deal of time in Persia, and we came
to know one another.
Richard You mean to say he's not a ghost?
Raoul He never has been, Father.
The Persian I was here when the chandelier fell. I knew him then. He is
very real.
Richard (*full of relief*) Not a ghost, after all? Why, that's ... that's —

Rémy screams, off

It's what, Rémy? (*He moves* UC) Good God! (*He moves* DL)
Raoul (*crossing* R, *fast*) He's vanished into thin air!
The Persian (*moving* DC, *taking out his pistol, fast*) Quick, man! For your
life! Put up your pistol! (*To Richard*) You too, sir!
Richard (*fed up*) I haven't got a pistol!
The Persian It doesn't matter. Hold the hand so! (*He leaps into the
position, facing front*) Ha!
Raoul (*leaping into the positon, facing front*) Ha!
Richard (*leaping into the position, facing front*) Ha!

Music. The Persian peers about him

The Persian (*softly, to Richard*) Our friend, you see, is an expert with the
Punjab Lasso.

Richard stares

Oh, yes.

He prowls and they do the same, staring nervously into the shadows. He moves up to the mirror

This is the room from which Miss Daaé disappeared, I believe ... (*He peers closer at the mirror moulding*) Aha!

He presses the same spot as Rémy. The same ripple of music, and the mirror swings open, the Persian reacting back against the wall, R. Rémy appears in the blackness without his lantern. Music

Richard Rémy!

Rémy walks slowly towards them

Rémy?

Rémy collapses onto his face, UC. There is the handle of a large dagger in his back. The music stops

Rémy!

He and Raoul kneel either side of Rémy, the Persian keeps half an eye on them, half an eye through the mirror, R, his gun at the ready

Raoul He's been stabbed! (*He peers closer*) Right through the heart.
The Persian At least it was quick and painless. This is rare where *he* is concerned.
Richard Poor Rémy. He was damned irritating, but he could be so — so—

He appeals to Raoul and the Persian, but they can only shrug. He rises

I don't know what your plans are, Mr Mysterious Persian, but count me in. I'll see this devil dead if it's the last thing I do.
Raoul Well said, Father.
The Persian (*peering off*) There are steps here, leading down. Very narrow, very steep. He can't be far below us.
Raoul (*crossing to snatch up his lantern*) Then let's get after him!

The Persian (*holding up a hand*) No, my young friend — after *me*. I know his little tricks. And remember — the hand always so. (*He gets into the position*) Ha!
Raoul (*into the position*) Ha!
Richard (*into the position*) Ha!
The Persian Very good.

Music. The Persian creeps off into the darkness

Raoul and Richard follow him, either side of the mirror, Raoul R, Richard L. Richard pauses and calls Raoul back

Richard Here, I say, Raoul ...

They return to peer round the mirror to one another

Are you sure we can — ?
Raoul Trust this Persian? What choice do we have, Father?

He goes, Richard pauses, looks back at Rémy. The music tender

Richard 'Efficient' ... that was the word.

Finger before nose, he goes, the Lights fading to black-out, a cymbal crescendo covering the change as the boxes truck on, the curtains fly in, and very dim Light builds to:

SCENE 3

Box Five

The stage and auditorium. Immediately following

Very dim light. During the change, Faust and Jammes, both carrying lanterns, have entered the auditorium and ascended the stage, moving to C, Faust leading the way

Faust Talk about Miss Daaé disappearing! Anybody could in this murk.

Madam Giry, carrying a lantern, appears between them suddenly, through the centre of the curtains

Madam Giry You two!

Jammes shrieks and runs round to Faust

What are you still doing here? Everybody else gave up and went home ages ago!
Faust We'd like to, but we can't find the way out.
Madam Giry (*pointing* R) Try going through the door marked Exit. (*As they move off*) It also says Gentlemen, but don't let that put you off.

They descend into the auditorium

And turn left at the end of the corridor — the right-hand stairs lead down to the cellars.
Faust Right you are. Left it is.

He cries out as he bangs his shin on the way out of an auditorium door

Madam Giry Useless great lump. If village idiots could sing, they'd all be tenors.

As she goes to follow them, there is a bump and a cry from the gallery

Who's that up there?
Dominique Dominique, Madam Giry, the Head Usherette. I'm lost, as well. Why doesn't Mauclair put some light on?
Madam Giry I'm just off down the cellars to sort him out. If I'm not mistaken, he'll be kipping in the boiler room.
Dominique How will I find my way out?
Madam Giry (*descending into the auditorium,* R) Follow your nose, dear. You'll probably end up in the bar, but that's nothing new.
Dominique Thank you very much, Madam Giry —

Madam Giry goes out of the auditorium door

— Miserable old bat. Still, she may have a point. This way, I think.

A loud bump, a cry and a sting. Light builds on Box Five

The Persian (*off, whispering*) Watch your heads. It's very low here.
Dominique What's that?
Richard (*off, whispering*) Secret passages in my opera house! Whatever next?

Another thud

Ow!
Raoul (*off, whispering*) What is it, Father?
Richard (*off, whispering*) It's very low here.
Dominique What's going on there?
The Persian (*off, whispering*) I've found some kind of lever. Take care. I'm going to pull it.

Music, and a creaking sound. A front panel of Box Five swings open, and a white-gloved hand appears. Dominique screams, running from the auditorium.The scream is kept going off down corridors for as long as possible. The hand withdraws

Richard (*off, whispering*) What the hell was that?
Raoul (*off, whispering*) God knows, but it sounded awful.
The Persian (*off, whispering*) Yes, gentlemen, your pistol hands. Ha!
Raoul (*off, whispering*) Ha!
Richard (*off, whispering*) Ha!

Music again, and the panel re-opens. Finger and gun before nose, Richard and Raoul poke their heads out. After a beat, the Persian's head rises up from the box, just his nose and eyes visible

Good Lord, we're back in the auditorium!

The Persian Yes — a secret passageway with an exit through the floor of Box Five. We now know how he managed Miss Daaé's disappearance from the stage.
Raoul And from her dressing-room.
Richard Up on the top floor. We're descending very rapidly.
Raoul She said he lives on the lake, and that's below the bottom cellar.

The Persian We must continue on down and let us pray we are in time.
I know this monster, and God knows what devilment he has in mind for
her — God knows.

*The Light fade quickly to Black-out as they withdraw back into the box.
Music, the boxes truck off. After one full figure is played, the curtains open
and continue on to fly out on:*

SCENE 4

Below the Bottom Cellar. The lake. Immediately following

Projecting on from UR, *a narrow wooden jetty with steps, and post. The
floor is covered with dry ice, and a mist hangs in the background. Ripples
play on everything. There is the sound of water, and of dripping, all
echoing. There is echo on all sound, speech and singing in this scene. The
music continues, sombre, beautiful. The elegant prow of the Phantom's
boat appears from extreme* UL. *Christine is draped over it on her back so
that we see her upturned face, her long hair falling into the water. The
Phantom rows, his back to us*

*He guides it slowly to the jetty, ships the oars, rises, lifts her, and steps up
on to the jetty. He puts her down slowly, and she looks about her, dazed,
uncomprehending, remembering nothing*

Christine (*seeing him*) You ... But why? ... Why? ... Where am I?

He crosses to her right, taking her by the hand, ready to lead her off

Raoul (*off, extremely faint*) Christine ...!

The Phantom reacts

Christine What is it?
Raoul (*off, extremely faint*) Christine ...!

The Phantom reacts again

Christine Did you hear something?

Softly, the Phantom places her against the post, and uses loose rope from it to bind her to it, her hands behind her back

What are you doing? ... I did as I promised.

He steps into the boat

I sang Marguerite for you one last time.

He pushes it off and rows across L

I don't understand why you're treating me this way ... Answer me ... Why won't you speak?

He steps from the boat on to the inside edge of the portal and begins to climb up, the boat continuing its drift off

Don't leave me ... where are you going? What are you going to do?

As high as he can go, he holds out a hand to her, then climbs off L and exits

Alone, Christine tugs at the bonds, looks about her. There is a long pause from her while the music continues

This awful place. (*She sings*)

Song 12: Somewhere Above the Sun Shines Bright

Christine   Somewhere above the sun shines bright
                          People stroll in the open air
                          Somewhere above in a summer sky
                          Birds spread their wings and fly
                          Lost and alone in endless night
                          Could one imagine so dire a plight?
                          In the darkness I cry like a child
                          Like a child I cry my lonely prayer
                          Somewhere above soft breezes blow
                          Clouds float in a lazy sky

Somewhere above me strangers meet
Lovers share a sigh
Lost and alone in endless night
Could one imagine so dire a plight?
In the darkness I cry like a child
Yes, like a child
My lonely prayer I cry
Ah! My, my prayer

The Lights fade to Black-out and the jetty trucks off R, *with Christine aboard. The boiler is set from extreme* UL *and the black cloth dropped in behind it, all very quickly. Lights build on:*

Scene 5

The Persian's Tale

The Boiler Room. Immediately following

The music dies. The boiler is huge and black, UC, *with two large round doors. Smoke from the last scene still drifts, and there is a loud hum. After a moment, Madam Giry enters from* L, *the lantern held high in the gloom. There is echo on all sound, dialogue and song in this scene*

Madam Giry (*crossing slowly* R) Mauclair! Are you in the boiler room?
   … If he's asleep again, I'll have his guts for garters … Mauclair!

To a huge sting, the body of Mauclair crashes at her feet from UR, *and she reacts with a scream. Recovering, holding out the lantern, she slowly approaches the body again*

   Mauclair? That's a bit of deep sleep, even for you.

A soft thud, and a yell, off. Music, continuing

Richard (*off*) Ah!
Raoul (*off*) Now what is it?
Richard (*off*) I hit my head again. It's some sort of metal handle.

Trying to find the source of the sound, Madam Giry moves L, *facing downstage. Behind her, the left-hand round door of the boiler slowly opens, music building. She turns, just in time to see a white-gloved hand emerge. She screams, recoiling* DL

Raoul (*off*) There's that awful noise again.

Richard's head appears from the boiler door and stares at Madam Giry

Richard No need to panic. I can see what it is. (*He climbs out, and looks back*) That's funny. It's an old boiler.
Madam Giry Do you mind?
Richard (*hastily*) No, Madam Giry, I was referring to this contraption, part of which is clearly a false door, out of which we have just extricated ourselves after a long and arduous journey down a secret passage which started all the way up in ... (*He gives up, and calls inside the boiler*) It's all right, it's only Madam Giry.
Raoul (*climbing out, the echo on his voice reducing as he does so*) What do you mean, only Madam Giry? Is there worse?

Madam Giry stares at him and he stiffens

Where are we, anyway?
Madam Giry The boiler room — *sir*.
Raoul Funny place for a secret passage to end up.
The Persian (*climbing out, the echo on his voice also reducing*) There will be another concealed entrance — one that takes us even lower. Look around.

His back to Mauclair, Raoul moves up the right side of the boiler. Having closed the door, the Persian turns to see Mauclair. He reacts, crossing to kneel, during the following

Richard (*to Madam Giry*) May I ask what you're doing here, madam?
Madam Giry I came down to sort out Mauclair, sir — (*she indicates*) but, as you can see, he's asleep again.
Richard (*turning to see him*) Oh, really!

He crosses to him, but the Persian holds up a warning hand and rattles off some dangerous sounding Persian gibberish

What?

The Persian repeats it exactly

Oh, I see.

The Persian His last sleep, I'm afraid. Delivered by the (*he appears to pluck something from the back of Mauclair's neck, the body twitching*)...Hyderabad Hypodermic.

Richard The what?

The Persian rises. Madam Giry and Raoul join Richard in peering at the Persian's nipped thumb and forefinger

The Persian An injection of deadly poison, administered by a dart, invisible to the naked eye.

He flicks his finger, and their eyes follow the trajectory of the invisible dart over and down to the floor L. *During the following all cross quickly* L, *holding lanterns, looking for it, still unable to see it*

Your 'ghost', madam, drugged Mauclair, and turned off the lights, every time he wished to bring off one of his little surprises ... (*He lifts Mauclair's legs*) ... but this time he has shut the poor fellow's mouth for good.

He drags Mauclair off, R. *The boiler hum, reduced, begins imperceptibly to fade out*

Madam Giry That foreign person wants to watch himself, sir. You know what happens to people who cross 'him'.

Richard Sadly, I do, Madam Giry. But this is not the work of a ghost. He is irrefutibly a man — a walking nightmare of a man.

The Persian enters, his voice strong

The Persian Yes, my friend ...

Eastern music underlays

You little realize how accurate a description you give. Nor is it surprising you took him for a ghost for I have known him a long time, this man you call 'The Phantom' ... Although in my country he is known under another title ... 'The King of the Trap Doors'.

Raoul 'The King of the Trap Doors'? Crikey!

The Persian Like myself, he has trained in the circus as a magician, and became an expert in hidden trap doors, and mechanical devices ... so much so that a certain Sultan not only employed him for the fiendish skill with which he created new engines of torture, but also had him design a whole new palace, cunningly fitted with secret passageways and doors — (*he moves to the boiler*) so that our Sultan could appear (*he opens the door*) and disappear (*he closes it*) at will ... adding a certain spice to his cruel pleasures. (*He goes close to them*) But for these to stay secret, the Phantom had to suffer the inevitable eastern consequence.

Richard Good God.

Raoul Filthy brutes.

Madam Giry tuts

The Persian Fortunately, I heard of this. (*He moves* R) I found him. I rescued him. And my reward ... (*he turns on them furiously, then controls himself*) I will only say that ever since that day, I have tracked him over many years. I had almost lost hope until I heard of the strange happenings here — and I knew that at last I had found the deformed creature.

Madam Giry Did you say deformed?

The Persian Oh yes, I knew those present at his birth. He is horribly disfigured. And yet his voice ...

He sings

Song 13: Born With a Monstrous Countenance

The Persian   Born with a monstrous countenance
                        No flesh on his face, his skull peeled white
                        A freak with the voice of an angel
                        Yet when he sang we fled from the sight

And so he masked himself
And travelled
A nightly apparition
Till dealing death in Persia
Became his sole ambition

One day the Sultan seized him
I fought to save his head
This kindness so displeased him
He left me there for dead

Fifteen years I've tracked him
And while I could find no trace
The Phantom was in the Opera house
Building a secret place

His private domain of darkness
Where all who saw him perished
Close to his world of music
The singing that he cherished
Safe but for one thing ...

A young girl called Christine Daaé
Sings and creates a pretty stir

Raoul moves towards him

He loses his heart and sees a way
He can pretend to be her Angel of Music
Until the day that he possesses her
Now he possesses her ...

Raoul moves quickly, brokenly, up to the boiler, his back to the action

The Phantom of the Opera
Possesses her

There is a long pause

Madam Giry (*gloomily*) All these years, and he wasn't even a proper ghost. I did everything for that man.

Richard (*patting her arm*) He fooled us all, Madam Giry. Don't be too downcast.

Madam Giry (*a bit surprised*) Thank you, sir. You're very kind.

The gaze into one another's eyes, sudden sparks flying in this strange, dark place. Raoul becomes aware of the pause, looks up and turns round

Raoul (*impatiently*) You two can make up later. Let's get on with it.

The Persian I agree. (*He indicates off* L) Those steps, Madam Giry — where do they lead?

Madam Giry (*turning to look, holding up her lantern*) Down to the bottom cellar, sir, but there's nothing down there now — it's empty.

Richard You said there was a manhole. (*To the others*) Down to the lake.

Raoul (*excited*) Is this true, Madam Giry?

Madam Giry Yes sir, but after they dropped them bodies down it, we had it blocked off.

Raoul Nevertheless, I'm going to take a look.

The Persian makes a move

No, you stay and search in here. She said she saw men working at boilers. I'll be all right.

The Persian Very well, but take great care. And remember ... (*he gets into the position*) Ha!

Raoul (*into the position*) Ha!

Richard (*into the position*) Ha!

Madam Giry (*into the position just as quickly, without quite knowing why*) Ha!

The others look about, puzzled to hear a fourth "ha!"

Raoul goes off L, *pistol in front of his nose, pausing to look oddly at Madam Giry*

The Persian (*indicating* R) We will begin the search over here.

He goes off R *with his pistol before his nose, Richard and Madam Giry go to follow him, their fingers held before their noses*

Richard You'd better stick very close to me, Madam Giry.

Madam Giry Are you sure that's quite proper, sir?

Richard It's all right, I'm a widower. (*As they go*) By the way, what do your friends call you?

Madam Giry (*as they go, sourly*) I haven't *got* any friends.

Music. Fast fade to Black-out. The black cloth flies out, the boiler trucks off L, *the manhole trucks on* R. *As the music fades, Light builds on:*

SCENE 6

The Punjab Lasso

The Bottom Cellar. Same time

The lighting is gloomy. Stone steps lead from high up, UL. *They have an iron railing, and a pale gas-lamp attached. The manhole,* R, *is stone, circular, like a well parapet, with a convex iron grille covering it. Ripples of water are cast from it, lighting the* R *upstage portal and the face of anybody who looks down into it*

Raoul cautiously enters down the steps, carrying his lantern, pistol before his nose. He moves slowly to C, *peering about him. There is a movement on the floor* DL, *and he turns swiftly, pointing the pistol — Ha! — and we see a furry shape scoot off into the* DL *entrance, squeaking. Recovering, he crosses to the well, puts his lantern on the floor behind it, peers down into the water, takes a coin from his pocket, drops it and listens. After an interval, there is a distant 'plop' and the ripples on his face speed up. He puts down the pistol, takes hold of the grille, and tugs with all his might, but it won't budge. He snatches up his pistol in frustration and moves* LC *to face upstage, his back dejected. A brief pause, then a thin, eerie, Eastern piping is heard, and the* DR *entrance begins to glow from within—a pale green light. He turns quickly to stare at this, then with a soft, 'ha!', he brings the pistol to his nose, and cautiously and slowly moves above the portal* R. *He takes a deep breath, then springs to face the entrance, pointing his pistol. The sound and the light instantly disappear. He peers off, puzzled, then turns, lowering the pistol, and moves onstage a couple of paces. There is a sharp whipping sound, and his head is jerked back. He drops the pistol and clutches at his throat, but is dragged partially off* DR, *to fight his way back onstage. We can now see the thin cord around his neck, leading off* DR. *He fights to reach the pistol, but is jerked back and on to his back. His feet slide off into the darkness, and the music—which has been strong and dramatic—fades to a throbbing drone*

There is a bang and a cry, off, and Faust appears on the stairs

Faust That's twice I've done that. It's ruining these tights. (*He descends*) Jammes, will you please try and keep up, or we'll never get out of here.

Jammes' head appears

Jammes We keep going down. (*She descends*) Are you sure Madam Giry said to turn right?
Faust (*peering off* L) Of course I'm sure! I'm always sure!
Jammes I thought she said left. (*She glances off* DR, *and leaps into the air with a piercing scream*) Aaah!
Faust (*jumping out of his skin*) What was that?
Jammes (*to him*) Me going, 'Aaah!'
Faust This is no time for footling jokes, woman!
Jammes It's no joke — (*she points*) — look!

The music rebuilds

Raoul reappears, on his knees, fighting his way back on stage

Faust screams

The Persian appears quickly at the top of the stairs and fires his pistol

Faust and Jammes scream, and Raoul collapses. The Persian hurries to him

The Persian My young friend, are you all right? (*He loses all sympathy as he sees the black cord around Raoul's neck*) The Punjab Lasso.

He takes it and lifts Raoul back to his feet, strangling

This is why I told you to keep your hand before your throat!

Raoul (*pulling it free*) Well, I'm very sorry!

Richard and Madam Giry appear at the head of the stairs

Richard Raoul!

Faust and Jammes scream

The Persian prowls off DR

Raoul picks up his pistol

Richard helps Madam Giry down into the cellar

Are you all right? What was all the shooting?
Raoul (*peering about*) It's him. He's here somewhere. He nearly got me.
Madam Giry (*going to Faust and Jammes*) I told you two to turn left, or
    you'd end up in the cellars!
Jammes (*to Faust*) See!
Raoul Just as well they didn't, Madam Giry. It was their screams saved
    me. (*He puts a hand on each of their shoulders*) Thanks, chaps.

The Persian returns

(*He turns to the Persian*) Did you ——

He finds Faust holding his hand

(*Having to pull his hand free*) Did you wing him?
The Persian There's no blood, no sign of anything. Only these blank
    walls.

He crosses to extreme UR *between the manhole and the group*

Raoul Damn the brute. He really *is* a ghost.

Raoul crosses to the manhole and shouts down

Damn you!

The Phantom (*off, echoing, as if from the well*) Damn ...you ...!

Raoul stiffens. Music. All believe this to be the echo of Raoul's voice

The Persian (*hurrying to him*) What is it? What do you see?

Raoul reaches a long way down into the manhole, straining, and fetches out a piece of white material

Richard It's a handkerchief!
Raoul Christine's. And still tear-stained.

Richard puts a hand on his shoulder

The Persian (*peering into the manhole*) Look there — those scratch marks.
Raoul (*joining him*) By George, they look like staves of music!
The Persian So they are. (*He thinks*) I wonder. A lock sprung to react to a certain pitch of sound ... it is possible. Can you sing it?
Raoul I'll have a bash.
The Persian Good lad.

Raoul sings down the manhole, his voice echoing, slowly moving round it in a circle, followed by the Persian, to end back where they started. Richard, Madam Giry, Faust and Jammes still in their group L, stare at them as if they are mad

Song 14 : In the Shadows, Dim and Dreary

Raoul	In the shadows, dim and dreary
	Unseen by all
	There's a secret hidden doorway
	Through solid wall
	Unlock on my command
	Unveil your mystery
The Persian	Go on, Raoul
	(*To the others*) I think it's working

The Others	(*Unimpressed*)
	Whoopee
Raoul	Yield to the force of love
	And turn the key

*A long pause, then the sound of a bolt and massive grinding of stone. Faust
yells, indicating steps behind him, and all run UR to stare as the steps
slowly grind their way upstage, hinging to reveal a hole from which pours
a green light. Music. Raoul gets to the front, crouching, peering in*

Richard (*staring in*) I don't believe it!

Raoul goes into the hole

Careful, Raoul!
The Persian (*crossing quickly to the hole*) Follow him! It's important we
stay together! (*To Faust and Jammes*) You two, as well!

He ducks into the hole

Faust (*interested*) Who's he?
Richard (*taking Madam Giry by the hand*) Oh, shut up and do as he says.

*As he leads Madam Giry to the hole, followed by Faust and Jammes, the
Light fades to Black-out. The music builds, then fades to a thin accompa-
niment. Their voices are heard, echoing, as in a tunnel*

Jammes (*off*) Oh Mr Faust! I can feel a draught.
Faust (*off*) Well, it's nothing to do with me, dear.
Richard (*off*) Just do as you're told, you two — and stick close to me and
Amelia.
Faust (*off*) *Amelia*?
Madam Giry (*off*) You heard him!
The Persian (*off, softly*) Quiet! I think we're getting somewhere.

A twittering of birds, and the Light builds on:

Scene 7

An Illusion in Iron

An underground room. Immediately following

*A strange, brilliant scene. At the rear, a cloth depicting a primitive jungle,
complete with animals, and some sky.* c, *a mound of foliage, with an ape
crouched in it, a serpent entwined around one of the branches.* R *and* L, *are
two spiky plants. The* DR *and* DL *entrances are shut off with barred gates,
through which shines a pale green light.* DC *is a small, golden casket. The
lighting is dappled and mysterious, the sounds are the sounds of an aviary,
not a jungle. Raoul crawls on from* R *followed by the Persian. Raoul moves
around the mound, from* L *to* R, *the Persian* DC. *Madam Giry crawls on*

Madam Giry (*staring*) Now what? (*She, too, moves around the mound
from* L *to* R)

Richard crawls on, crosses to the plant, L *then Jammes crawls on*

Jammes Ooh!

She runs to peer through the bars DL

Faust enters, remaining on his hands and knees, peering about

Faust Are we outside?
Madam Giry Don't be ridiculous. We're five storeys underground.

She joins Richard, L

The Persian It is one of his illusions.
Jammes An illusion?
The Persian (*crossing up to the mound,* L) I have experienced this one
before. An exotic torture chamber, similar to one he designed for the
Sultan.

He taps a soft-looking leaf with his gun, and it clanks

Raoul Iron!

Music rumbles, the birds become distorted. Raoul moves quickly to the bars, R, tapping them. Jammes taps hers. Madam Giry feels the portal, L, Richard, the cloth, Faust, the floor. The Persian moves around the mound, above to its right

The Persian Everything you see will be made of the same metal. The Sultan used to call it his 'African Forest'.
Richard Why did he do that?
The Persian Because the iron can be heated to a tropical heat. Red heat, if necessary. The heat of an oven.

He sees the casket and moves slowly towards it during the following, followed by all the others to form a tight group around him, DC

But his victims need not perish from the heat, for it was part of the torture to offer them the choice of a quicker death ... (*he opens the casket*) ... the Punjab Lasso.

He holds up a tangle of black cord. Sting in the music

Six. And six of us.

With a great screech of metal, a wall drops in behind them. It is the 'corridor' cloth, but completely unlit. The Lighting almost a full Black-out except for a pale blue glimmer on their figures

The music continues to rumble

Fool that I am, we are trapped!

As they peer about them, panic-stricken, the echoing laugh of the Phantom is heard. They freeze

Richard (*whispering*) Is it him again?
The Persian No doubt he is watching us — as he and the Sultan used to watch the sufferings of those other tortured wretches in Persia.
Richard Well, do something! You got us in here, get us out!

The Persian I will try what I can, but I fear it is useless.

He moves to LC and calls up

Phantom ... Remember me, Phantom! ... Remember the Circus ... and remember — our mother!

Sting in the music. All react away from him

The Phantom (*off*) I'm afraid you call in vain, my little brother. You chose your path, I mine. You may now perish with your friends. I would compose you all a requiem, but time presses — you must die unaccompanied. Adieu.

The music has died, and a soft hissing takes over, building in intensity. Everything begins to glow red, and all stagger and pull at their throats as the heat hits them

The Persian It is as I feared. He is beyond reason. He has turned on the heat.

He breaks up LC, beaten

Faust (*tearful*) He could have at least let me go!
Madam Giry Oh, really!
Raoul Buck up, man.
Faust Well! All I did was take a wrong turning (*to Jammes*) and that was your fault!
Richard Recriminations are pointless. Leave the child be.

Raoul holds out his hand and Jammes runs to him to be comforted

(*To Madam Giry*) Are you all right, Amelia?
Madam Giry (*gasping*) I think so, Emile ... Only it's so hot ... Can't get me breath ...
The Persian (*holding up the lassos*) Yes, we may be glad of these soon.
Raoul I'll never take that way out.
Richard (*proudly*) Nor I. We can at least die like Frenchmen.
Faust (*bitterly*) We're *going* to die like Frenchmen ... beautifully cooked!

They sing. The lighting is now quite bright, although extremely red. They sing more or less in a line, out front, grand opera. Raoul and Jammes are R, the Persian and Faust L, Richard and Madam Giry C

Song 15: What an Awful Way to Perish

Faust

What an awful way to perish
Such a dreadul ending lies in store
He's cremating us
Annihilating us
Burnt alive!
Six little piles of cinders glowing
There'd be five
But I was slow in getting going
To survive
We'd have to have a way of knowing
How to thrive
Inside an oven so red-hot
It's bound to melt the fillings in your teeth

The Persian

What an awful way to perish
Such a dreadul ending lies in store
He's cremating us
Annihilating us
Burnt alive!
Six small piles a-glowing
There'd be five
But I was slow getting going
To survive
We'd have to have a way of knowing
How to thrive
Inside an oven
Hot enough to melt
The fillings in your teeth

Madam Giry

Oh Emile, how appalling
Now we'll never ever know for sure
Was it meant to be?
Were you sent to me?
Burnt alive!
Our ashes mingling in a tender way

Love survives
No matter what the Phantom has to say
It arrived
And though it's not a very happy day
Never mind
For although we're going to suffer
I know I'll be with you
When I am burnt alive

Richard
Oh Amelia, how appalling
Now we'll never ever know
Was it meant to be?
Were you sent to me?
Burnt alive!
Our ashes mingling
Love survives
No matter what the Phantom has to say
It arrived
And though it's not a very happy day
Never mind
I'll be with you
You and me both burnt alive

Faust
It's so awful
While I'm so young
So young still
There is such a lot still inside me
There are so many roles left unsung
It's awful
Wrong for me to burn alive

The Persian
It's so awful
It's so awful
And how I hate him
Hate him so
But I've lost
I'll never know revenge
There's no escape
Not a hope
So soon we'll all be burning

Madam Giry
Oh, my dear Emile
Can't get me breath, sir

There's no air
Ah! Ah! Ah!
There's no oxygen left
We'll all suffocate now
And so goodbye, sir
I'll say goodbye
Goodbye

Jammes   Oh I feel it all, it's all aglow
So red
It's really glowing
Nearly going
Really going red
I can't go on no more
So goodbye
I can't go on
Goodbye

Faust   No! Oh no! Oh no! Oh no!
Oh no! Can't go on
I'm done
I'm done
Ready to say
Farewell and goodbye
At least we die like Frenchmen
Goodbye

Raoul   Oh, I feel it all, it's all a glow
So red it now begins to show
The heat, the heat, it's burning
This unbearable dreadful awful heat
Now we'll never save Christine
So farewell, my friends, goodbye
At least we die like Frenchmen
Goodbye

The Persian   Ah! I can feel it, a terrible glow
Ah! Ah! The heat, it's beginning to show
Fate is ours as Allah wills it
And Allah wills that we shall die
So farewell, friends, goodbye
Goodbye

Richard	Ah! The heat, it's beginning to show
	It's such unbearable terrible heat
	Oh!
	No more air
	So now goodbye
	Goodbye

*By now, all are on their knees. As they sing the final note, they collapse —
Jammes doing a dying swan — and Lights fade to Black-out, the hissing
building to a loud level over the scene-change. Some of the voices in the
above song can be doubled from off if necessary from 'Oh my dear Emile'.
The company clear, taking the casket with them. The gates hinge open, and
the cloth rises on:*

SCENE 8

The Final Drama

The Phantom's Chapel. Immediately following

*Although the lighting is subdued, everything seems to glow. At the rear,
the huge pipes of the organ (backlit cloth) with keyboard and lighted
candelabra below. Above, purple drapes and glowing chandeliers. The
music tinkles and rustles. The Phantom enters from R, followed more
slowly by Christine. There is a little echo on his voice only*

The Phantom (*taking off his hat*) Don't be frightened. I mean you no
harm.

Christine (*looking about her*) What place is this?

The Phantom (*taking off his cloak*) My chapel. (*He puts the hat and cloak
on to the organ,* L) The last time I brought you down, you came only to
the shores of my lake. Well, this time — this time, I do not think you will
be returning.

Christine I don't understand why you're doing this. I sang Marguerite.
That was my promise — to sing Marguerite for you one last time.

The Phantom (*moving* DL) But you did not sing it for *me*, Christine.

Christine (*faltering*) I swear it.

The Phantom Not in your heart. I think we both know for whom you sang.

She lowers her eyes

Well, all that is ended. Now you can only be mine.
Christine (*frightened*) What do you mean? What have you done? (*She crosses to him in sudden panic*) Raoul!
The Phantom (*crossing* R, *almost screaming*) Forget that name!
Christine (*to* C) What have you done to him? Tell me!
The Phantom He came between us. Well, no longer. I have destroyed him — utterly. He is dust.
Christine (*faltering*) You're lying to me.
The Phantom It is the truth, Christine. He is dead.

A pause. She sways, then falls. Music underlays the following. He half crosses to her

(*Softly, pained*) Oh, Christine … if only you could weep for me like that.
Christine (*muffled*) I did weep for you once.
The Phantom Out of pity, Christine, not love. But it is only a question of time. In time, you will grow to love me. I know it.

The music has stopped. He begins singing, unaccompanied

Song 16: Ne'er Forsake Me, Here Remain

The Phantom   Ne'er forsake me, here remain
                        Share with me my dark domain
                        Beautiful flower of maidenkind
                        Here in the bower where our love's enshrined
                        Give me your loving care
                        Oh free me from this dark despair
                        Tender scion of Philomel
                        Here in the shadows weave your magic spell
                        My maid of music, weave your magic spell
                        Why don't you swear here to join me
                        Where I can call you mine forever?
                        Oh, my Christine …
                        Ne'er forsake me, here remain
                        Share with me my dark domain
                        Beautiful flower of maidenkind

Here in the bower where our love's enshrined
Here in the shadows weave your magic spell
My gentle maiden, weave your magic spell
Here in the shadows weave your spell

The last note turns into a sustained high falsetto scream, the Phantom leaning over her, nearer and nearer. It should last as long as possible. Finally she pulls off the white mask, and the scream turns into a terrible cry, the Phantom turning and crawling away from her DR, the music thundering, screaming in its turn, the lighting changing to one very harsh, bright, low spotlight on his face, spilling on Christine beyond. As described by the Persian, his face is like a skull, the white bones jutting. After a while, he speaks, not looking at her

The Phantom (*in a low harsh voice, treated if possible*) So, Christine ... Do you hate me now? ... Do you? ... Hate me for being born a monster?
Christine No. I pity you, my poor Phantom, but love you, never. Your monster's face has soured your soul.

The bright Light fades, the other Lights return to normal, all effects and music cease. He rises and scoops up the mask, Christine recoiling

The Phantom Well. You have spoken. (*He crosses UL of the organ, to put down his mask carefully*) And now for the wedding ceremony.
Christine (*rising and recoiling DL*) What?
The Phantom I had hoped for a more joyous occasion, but one must do what one must. We shall be properly married here — you and I.

He has pressed an organ key. Music: 'Ne' er forsake me'. Very slowly, the wedding dress, on a dressmaker's former, glides on from R. Light glows on it. He waits until it is fully on and still before speaking

Put it on.
Christine Never.
The Phantom Christine, put — it — on!

He points a finger. The music becomes hypnotic. With a dead face, she moves stiffly towards the wedding dress, following it as it retreats into the darkness R, the Phantom following her with his finger

Soon, we shall be united, Christine — forever!

He flings himself at the organ and plays the opening of the Bach toccata and fugue at full throttle, his elbows working, his coat-tails flapping. After the introduction, he jumps up to the left of the organ, and points a finger at it. It continues to play quietly on its own

We shall reign side by side, my dearest Christine — side by side in my domain of darkness — never moving, never tiring — side by side — forever!

He produces a long, gleaming knife, holding it up high. Music crashes and the organ stops. The lighting changes to a down light on him, and a sidelight on the knife. He turns it so that its light flashes over all the auditorium

I know she will never love me in life ... But in death ... Yes ... in death, there is time ... (*He caresses the knife lovingly*) All the time in the world...

Music and an area R begins to glow. He turns away, hiding the knife, as Christine slowly enters from R, wearing the wedding dress. He turns to stare at her

Oh, my goddess ... my diva ... (*He crosses and kneels before her*) Sing for me one last time ... I implore you ... As your teacher, I command you ... Sing!

The music stops

Christine (*dead voice*) I can never sing again.

A pause. He rises

The Phantom Then let the wedding ceremony commence. (*He takes her and leads her quickly over L*) It is time.
Christine What, no priest, no witnesses? Or is the ceremony also to be an illusion?
The Phantom No. The plans are laid.

*He presses another organ key. Snap to Black-out. The wooden thump of
an opening trapdoor. Two falling yells, becoming louder. A thump. A
special square downlight picks up the Priest and Chorus Girl, R. Sawdust
falls down the light*

Chorus Girl (*struggling up*) Oh, me bruises! (*She looks up into the trap
light*) What happened to the pavement?

*As she helps up the Priest, the lighting reverts to normal and they both see
the Phantom. Both scream and recoil*

The Phantom Don't be alarmed. All will become clear shortly. (*Aside*)
And afterwards, there will be no need of explanation.
The Priest I say, it's powerful stuff, this beaujolais. I've only had six
litres, and I'm hallucinating.
The Phantom It's quite real, Parson. You are simply to officiate a
wedding. Your 'friend' is our witness. Do you have a prayer-book?
The Priest Not on me.
Chorus Girl He's been ministering all night.
The Phantom (*pointing above, furious*) Then you may use mine!

A large prayer-book falls from above, landing at the priest's feet

The Priest (*picking it up, to the Chorus Girl*) This is the weirdest dream.
Pinch me, and I'll wake up.
Chorus Girl You don't, usually.
The Phantom Perform the ceremony! (*He leads Christine forward*) And
allow me to introduce my bride.
The Priest Charmed, I'm sure. (*To the Chorus Girl*) I think it's going to
be all right. (*He moves* UC, *to the Phantom*) If you'd care to kneel.

*The Phantom and Christine kneel, facing upstage, before him. Seeing this,
the Chorus Girl also kneels*

Not you!
Chorus Girl (*rising, angry*) Well, how was I to know? I've only been
consummated, not married!
The Phantom Silence! ... And proceed.

He waves a hand. Soft, nuptial organ music

The Priest (*opening the book*) 'Dearly beloved, we are gathered here today in the sight of God to join together this woman and this — in Holy Matrimony. (*He leans forward, confidentially to the Phantom*) I take it you just want the short version?
The Phantom (*a dangerous growl*) Hurry up.
The Priest (*recoiling*) Do you have a ring?

The Phantom holds it high in his left hand

Place it on her finger.

The Phantom does so

I now pronounce you man and —

The Persian enters quickly from DL, *covering him with his pistol*

The Persian Oh, no, you don't!

Chord, and the organ stops

Madam Giry enters R, *pointing*

Madam Giry Don't you dare!

Chord

Richard enters L, *pointing*

Richard Don't move, Phantom!

Chord

Raoul enters DR, *covering him with his pistol*

Raoul All the exits are covered!

A chord

Faust and Jammes run on from L, to be upstage of Madam Giry

Christine (*rising*) Raoul, you're alive!

Final chord as she runs to him

The Phantom (*screaming*) Alive! Impossible! You can't have escaped!
You can't! How did you do it?
Richard It was really rather simple, Phantom. Somebody turned off the
gas.

He gestures

*Rémy, his arm in a sling enters from L, to stand proudly on Richard's left.
A fanfare, ending on a rather cracked note*

The Phantom You!
Richard He was badly wounded, Phantom, but you failed to kill him, for
Rémy is one of those rare people with his heart on the — erm — on the
— erm—
Rémy (*irritated*) Other side, sir.

The Phantom makes as if to attack them

*Two Stagehands appear upstage of Richard and Rémy, carrying pick-
axe handles, followed by Lisette, carrying a lantern*

The Phantom turns away R to stare at Christine

The Persian And now, little brother, you must answer to me. There is one
tale of your infamy I did not relate — the murder of our mother and
father! ... I knew they never fell off that tight-rope! You greased it, you
horror!
The Phantom They knew me for what I am! Nobody must live who sees
my face!

*He draws out the word 'face', moving in a big semi-circle from R to L,
driving them all back, to be faced by the Persian, who drives him back in
his turn with the pistol*

The Persian Which is why you sought my death in Persia! I live to this
day only because you thought your assassin succeeded! And now —(*he
cocks the pistol*) — the final drama.
Christine (*running forward*) No!
Raoul Christine!

But he is too late, The Phantom has grabbed Christine, the knife held high

The Phantom Don't move! I can kill her and myself before any of you
move!

*He moves her R and L, always keeping her between him and pistols of the
Persian and Raoul, neither seeing the opportunity for a clear shot. Music
underlays all the following*

Chorus Girl (*running RC*)Oh Mum, I swear I'll never touch another drop!

*The Phantom slashes at the Chorus Girl with the knife. She screams, and
the Priest drags her back*

The Phantom (*soft, pained*) Oh, Christine ... even my last happiness is
to be denied me ... We must die unwed.
Raoul No! (*He puts down the pistol, holding out his hands*) Please.
Madam Giry (*moving in a little*) Don't do it, sir.

*The Phantom looks at her, his staunch supporter through the years. A
pause*

The Phantom Remember ... I do this out of love ... I am not all monster
... Farewell ... Christine ...

*He stabs, the motion concealed by her body. Big sting in the music.
Everybody turns away, crying out in horror. A pause, then Christine pulls
free and runs to Raoul. She is unharmed. All turn to stare at the Phantom.
We now realize he has stabbed himself instead. He pulls out the knife,
drops it and falls*

Christine ... All I ever did was love ... Christine.

The music stops. As before, he begins the song, unaccompanied. During it, light focuses on him

Song 17: Ne'er Forsake Me, Here Remain (Reprise)

The Phantom	Ne'er forsake me, here remain
	Share with me my dark domain
	Beautiful flower of maidenkind
	Here in the bower where our love's enshrined
Christine	Give me your loving care
The Phantom	Oh free me from this dark despair
Christine	Tender scion of Philomel
	Here in the shadows weave
The Phantom	Tender scion of Philomel
	Here in the shadows weave your magic spell
	My gentle maiden, weave your magic ...

Silence. He dies. The music returns as Christine takes off the ring, presses it into his dead hand. Raoul moves forward, and brings her back, R

The Persian Well, at least he's at rest now.
Richard Poor —
Rémy Devil?
Richard Yes. Bit of good in him somewhere, I suppose.
Raoul There is in us all, Father, there is in us all.
The Priest Amen to that.
Christine And he was once my Angel of Music.

All face front and sing:

Song 18: He Will Not Go Without a Friend

All	He will not go without a friend
	Will not go without a friend
	Without a friend
	Without a friend
	And so we end

Black-out. Restore lighting for curtain calls. The calls are taken separately downstage of the tableau curtain, which closes as soon as possible, and which resemble 'Opera' calls as much as possible. The Phantom is the last to appear, wearing his hat and white mask. He turns upstage and sweeps off the hat and mask. The Company react back in horror, but when he turns front it is the actor, the hideous make-up removed

CURTAIN

GROUND PLAN

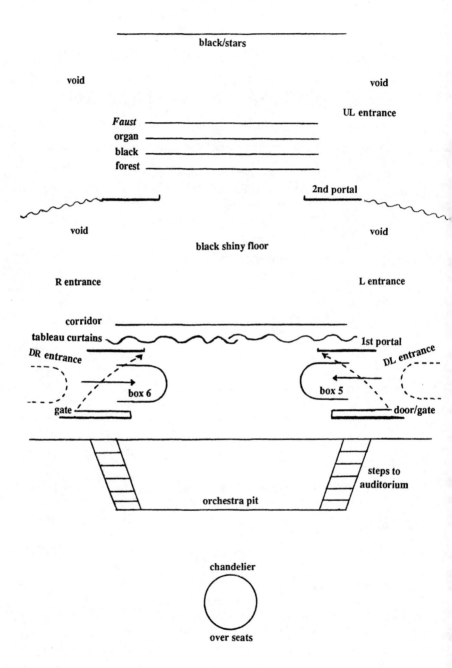

black/stars

void

void

UL entrance

Faust

organ

black

forest

2nd portal

void

void

black shiny floor

R entrance

L entrance

corridor

tableau curtains

1st portal

DR entrance

DL entrance

box 6

box 5

gate

door/gate

steps to
auditorium

orchestra pit

chandelier

over seats

FURNITURE AND PROPERTY LIST

ACT I
SCENE 1

On stage: Tall pair of wooden step-ladders
Couple of paint-spattered chairs
Pots of paint and brushes
Two chairs in Box Five and Box Six

Off stage: White rose (**Stage Management**)
Ledger, pencil (**Rémy**)
Fan (**Carlotta**)

Personal: **Jammes**: reticule
Richard: cane
Rémy: glasses
Raoul: cane, white rose as a buttonhole, watch (*worn throughout*)

SCENE 2

On stage: Large ornate gothic chair and table. *On it*: tomes, scrolls, skull, faded
long-stemmed red rose, blue poison bottle, goblet
Two programmes in pocket in Box Five
Two programmes on chairs in Box Six
Two pairs of binoculars on chairs in Box Six

Off stage: Fan (**Carlotta**)
2 Pairs of binoculars (**Madam Giry**)

Personal: **Mephistopheles**: note

SCENE 3

On stage: Nil

SCENE 4

On stage: Hatstand with a garment hanging from it
Large potted plant

Small dressing-table and chair
Crushed white rose
Large mirror

SCENE 5

On stage: Keyhole desk. *On it*: letters, quill pen in a inkwell
                 Three chairs

Off stage: Letter (**Madam Giry**)
                 Glass of water (**Rémy**)

Personal: **Richard**: gloves, cane

SCENE 6

On stage: Nil

SCENE 7

On stage: A number of headstones
                 One large headstone and grave

Off stage: Small posy of white roses (**Christine**)
                 Pebble (**Phantom**)
                 Spade (**Gravedigger**)
                 Lantern (**Gravedigger**)

SCENE 8

On stage: Nil

Off stage: Spray (**Lisette**)
                 Music case (**Christine**)

Personal: Fan (**Carlotta**)
                 White handkerchief (**Faust**)

SCENE 9

On stage: Two chairs
                 Iron candelabra hanging on chains
                 Large ornate jewel box. *In it*: glittering necklaces, hand mirror
                 Key

SCENE 10

On stage: Nil

Off stage: Letter (**Madam Giry**)

Personal: **Richard**: piece of paper

SCENE 11

On stage: Huge statue of Apollo
                Balustrades

Off stage: Bird seed (**Old Man**)
                Dummy (**Phantom**)

ACT II
SCENE 1

On stage: Low palliasse

Off stage: Lanterns (**Extras, Richard, Raoul, Rémy**)
                Tray. *On it:* tea things (**Madam Giry**)
                Tiny table (**Jammes**)

Personal: **Faust**: ring

SCENE 2

On stage: Hatstand with a garment hanging from it
                Large potted plant
                Small dressing-table and chair
                Large mirror

Off stage: Lanterns (**Raoul, Rémy, Richard**)

Personal: **Persian**: two pistols, cigarette, trick lighted match
                Rémy: dagger and harness, split coat

SCENE 3

On stage: Nil

Off stage: Lanterns (Faust, Jammes, Madam Giry)

Personal: Persian: gun
                 Raoul: gun

                        SCENE 4

On stage: Narrow wooden jetty with steps and a post with some rope tied to it

Off stage: Boat with oars

                        SCENE 5

Strike: Jetty
                 Rope

Set: Boiler

Personal :   Raoul: pistol, lantern
                 The Persian: pistol
                 Madam Giry: lantern
                 Richard: lantern

                        SCENE 6

Strike: Boiler

Set: Manhole. *In it*: white handkerchief
                 Rat and line

Off stage: Lantern (Faust)
                 Thin black cord (Stage Management)

Personal: Raoul: pistol, coin in his pocket, lantern
                 Persian: pistol

                        SCENE 7

Strike: Manhole

Set: Central mound
                 Two spiky metal plants
                 Small golden casket. *In it*: tangle of black cord

Personal: **Raoul**: gun
               Persian: gun

SCENE 8

On stage :   Organ
               Bench
               Lighted candelabra
               Glowing chandeliers

Off stage: Dressmaker's former with wedding dress
               Large prayer-book
               Pick-axe handles (**Stage Hands**)
               Lantern (**Lisette**)

Personal: **Phantom**: long gleaming knife, wedding ring
               Persian: pistol
               Raoul: pistol
               Rémy: arm sling

LIGHTING PLOT

Practical fittings required: chandelier, sconces and candelabra
Various interior and exterior settings

ACT I, SCENE 1
To open: Long shaft of "working light" builds along the floor from UL
followed by a dim acting area

Cue 1	**Richard**: "... turn on some light!" *Bright lights build*	(Page 2)
Cue 2	**Madam Giry**: " It was the ghost— sir." *Lighting checks a little*	(Page 12)
Cue 3	Music crashes out *Fade quickly to black-out with final spot on Christine's face*	(Page 18)

ACT I, SCENE 2
To open: Curtains are warmly lit as are both boxes, the chandelier
at a low level

Cue 4	Prelude begins *Fade lights, a little light remaining on the two boxes*	(Page 19)
Cue 5	The curtain rises *Build on* Faust *scene*	(Page 19)
Cue 6	**Debienne**: "More light here!" *Build bright light*	(Page 21)
Cue 7	**Richard** and **Rémy** leave the auditorium. Music *Fade to black-out*	(Page 23)

ACT I, SCENE 3
To open: Gloomy lighting. Yellow light showing through the fan
above the door to the dressing-room. Sconces glow dimly

Cue 8	**Christine**: "I was going to sing tonight" *Shadows flit across the fanlight and Raoul's face*	(Page 24)

Cue 9 **Christine:** "I will know that." 3rd time (Page 24)
     Light in fanlight goes out

Cue 10 **Raoul** whistles and goes R (Page 25)
     Fast fade to black-out

ACT I, Scene 4
To open: Christine's dressing-room dimly lit

Cue 11 **Raoul** hurries off L (Page 26)
     *Lighting in the room checks sharply, building upstage of
      the mirror with a little light on the door to Christine's
      dressing-room*

Cue 12 **The Phantom** disappears upstage (Page 26)
     Revert to opening state

Cue 13 **Raoul** hurls the rose to the floor and goes R (Page 27)
     Fast lighting change

Cue 14 **Raoul** turns and strides off. Music finishes (Page 28)
     Snap to black-out

ACT I, Scene 5
To open: Bright and airy effect on Richard's office

Cue 15 **Groom** snaps his fingers (Page 32)
     Fade quickly. Snap on follow spot on Groom

Cue 16 **Groom** finishes in same snapped-finger pose (Page 33)
     Revert to previous lighting

Cue 17 **Richard:** " ...believe anything." Scrape and music (Page 35)
     *Light checks swiftly to a tight bright special on desk
      and two dimmer ones on Richard and Raoul*

Cue 18 Scrape. Music stops, the hand sinking out of sight (Page 36)
     Revert to previous lighting

Cue 19 **Raoul:** "But Father — Father!" Music (Page 37)
     Fast fade to black-out

ACT I, Scene 6
To open: Well-lit corridor

Cue 20	**Richard**: (*off*) "Which way is it?" Music *Lighting checks*	(Page 38)
Cue 21	**Jammes** flies off L *Fade to black-out*	(Page 39)

ACT I, SCENE 7
To open: Exterior lighting

Cue 22	**Christine**: "That I feel is there?" *A shadow flits across Christine's face*	(Page 40)
Cue 23	Sound of thin, cold wind, and high strings *Shafts of light break through the clouds striking down* *into the graveyard*	(Page 42)
Cue 24	**The Phantom**: "We'll share paradise" *Slowly restore normal lighting*	(Page 42)
Cue 25	**Raoul**: "Come back!" Music finishes. Owl hoots *Dim lights*	(Page 43)
Cue 26	**Raoul** runs off UL. Music *Fade to black-out*	(Page 44)

ACT I, SCENE 8
To open: Brightly lit corridor

Cue 27	Sombre music from the orchestra takes over *Lighting checks*	(Page 51)
Cue 28	**Madam Giry**: "God knows." *Fade quickly to black-out*	(Page 51)

ACT I, SCENE 9
To open: Interior lighting

Cue 29	**Richard**: "... Jewel Song for us." Music begins *Fade lights, a little light remaining on the two boxes*	(Page 52)
Cue 30	The curtain rises *Build on* Faust *scene*	(Page 52)

Cue 31   **Phantom: "...** to bring down the chandelier."   (Page 55)
            Build chandelier brightly

Cue 32   **Carlotta** looks at the iron candelabra above her head   (Page 55)
            Snap off lights except two tiny specials angled upwards
               to light only the candelabra

Cue 33   Iron candelabra drops   (Page 55)
            Black-out using black-out cards. Pause. Lighting restores

Cue 34   All stare at Faust   (Page 55)
            Snap to black-out

ACT I, SCENE 10
To open: Interior lighting

Cue 35   **Richard** goes. Music becomes sinister   (Page 58)
            Lighting checks

Cue 36   As **Rémy** goes to run off R   (Page 58)
            Fade to black-out

ACT I, SCENE 10
To open: Exterior lighting. Nightime

Cue 37   The **Phantom** jumps off the statue   (Page 63)
            Check lighting

Cue 38   Timpani roll and the **Phantom** runs DC   (Page 63)
            Snap on spot on Phantom

Cue 39   Music finishes   (Page 63)
            Fade to black-out

Cue 40   The curtain flies in   (Page 63)
            House lights and chandelier build to full

ACT II, SCENE 1
To open: Interior lighting. Evening. Lights build on curtains and boxes

Cue 41   **Richard: "...**that's all I can say." Music   (Page 64)
            Fade lights, a little light remaining on the two boxes

Cue 42   The curtain rises   (Page 65)
             Build on Faust *scene*

Cue 43   **Faust** springs from L   (Page 65)
             Build bright light

Cue 44   As **Faust** and **Christine** hit their top notes   (Page 67)
             Snap to black-out for 3 seconds; revert to opening state

Cue 45   **Raoul**: "…disappeared!" Timpani roll   (Page 68)
             Flicker lights, then almost go out, a dim downlight
             *   on Raoul*

Cue 46   The curtain falls   (Page 68)
             Bring up very dim light

Cue 47   **Jammes** hurries through the split   (Page 70)
             Soft follow spot on **Jammes**

Cue 48   **Madam Giry** appears through the split   (Page 70)
             Snap on follow spot on Madam Giry

Cue 49   **Madam Giry** turns sharply front   (Page 72)
             Snap off follow spot, together with snap to black-out

ACT II, SCENE 2

To open: Interior lighting

Cue 50   **Richard** exits   (Page 77)
             Fade to black-out

ACT II, SCENE 3
To open: Very dim light

Cue 51   A loud bump, a cry and a sting   (Page 79)
             Build light on Box 5

Cue 52   **The Persian**: "… God knows."   (Page 80)
             Fast fade to black-out

ACT II, SCENE 4
To open: Cavern lighting. Ripple effect. Evening

Cue 53   **Christine:** "Ah! My, my prayer"   (Page 82)
             Fade to black-out

ACT II, Scene 5
To open: Interior lighting. Evening

Cue 54   **Madam Giry:** "I haven't *got* any friends." Music   (Page 88)
             Fast fade to black-out

ACT II, Scene 6
To open: Gloomy interior. Ripple effect

Cue 55   A distant "plop"   (Page 88)
             Ripple effect speeds up

Cue 56   Eastern piping is heard   (Page 88)
             DR *entrance glows green*

Cue 57   **Raoul** springs to face entrance   (Page 88)
             Cut light

Cue 58   Steps hinge to reveal hole   (Page 92)
             Green light from hole

Cue 59   **Richard** leads **Madam Giry** to the hole   (Page 92)
             Fade to black-out. Then build for Scene 7

ACT II, Scene 7
To open: Dappled and mysterious lighting. Pale green light shining
             through barred gates DL and R. Evening

Cue 60   A wall drops in behind them   (Page 94)
             *Snap to black-out except for a pale blue glimmer on their
                 figures*

Cue 61   **Faust:** "... beautifully cooked!"   (Page 95)
             Bright, extremely red lighting

Cue 62   All are on their knees. They collapse   (Page 99)
             Fade to black-out

ACT II, Scene 8
To open: Subdued lighting. Interior. Glowing effect on everything

Cue 63   **The Phantom** crawls away from **Christine** DR   (Page 101)
            Very harsh bright low spotlight on the Phantom's face,
            spilling on Christine beyond

Cue 64   Christine: "... soured your soul."   (Page 101)
            Bright light fades. Revert to previous lighting

Cue 65   Wedding dress on a dressmaker's former glides on   (Page 101)
            Light glows on the wedding-dress

Cue 66   **The Phantom** produces a long, gleaming knife   (Page 102)
            Bring up a down light on the Phantom and a side light
            on the knife

Cue 67   **The Phantom:** "... in the world..." Music   (Page 102)
            An area R *begins to glow*

Cue 68   **The Phantom** presses another organ key   (Page 103)
            Snap to black-out

Cue 69   Two falling yells, becoming louder. A thump   (Page 103)
            Snap on special square downlight on **Priest** *and*
            Chorus Girl

Cue 70   **Chorus Girl** helps up the **Priest**   (Page 103)
            Revert to normal lighting

Cue 71   **The Phantom:** " ... was love ... Christine"   (Page 106)
            Music stops. Focus on **The Phantom** *while he sings*

Cue 72   All: "And so we end"   (Page 107)
            Snap to black-out. Restore lighting for curtain calls

EFFECTS PLOT

ACT I

Cue 1   **Christine:** " ...Sing for me ... " A long pause   (Page 42)
           Thin cold wind

Cue 2   Music finishes on a sinister note   (Page 43)
           An owl hoots

Cue 3   **Raoul:** " I'd better think." Pause   (Page 43)
           *Sudden grating sound, echoing, gradually becoming a thin
               rustling*

Cue 4   **Gravedigger:**" Well, he came to the right place.'   (Page 44)
           Galloping horse from the rear of the auditorium

Cue 5   **Gravedigger:** " ...straight for the wall."   (Page 44)
           Break in horse's hooves

Cue 6   When ready   (Page 44)
           Fade horse's hooves

Cue 7   To open SCENE 8   (Page 45)
           Tuning-up noises

Cue 8   **Jammes, Lisette, Rémy** and **Stage Hands** hurry on   (Page 46)
           Cut tuning-up noises

Cue 9   **Richard** reappears from L   (Page 51)
           Tuning-up noises

Cue 10   **Richard** goes DR, jauntily   (Page 51)
           Cut tuning-up noises

Cue 11   **Carlotta** enters   (Page 52)
           Audience applause, cut on her gesture

Cue 12   Music cue   (Page 54)
           Toad croaks

Cue 13	Music cue *Toad croaks*	(Page 54)
Cue 14	Music cue *Toad croaks twice*	(Page 54)
Cue 15	**Richard:** " The chandelier!" *Hacksawing, tinkling of crystal*	(Page 55)
Cue 16	**The Phantom:** (*off*) "No!" All stop *Cut hacksawing*	(Page 55)
Cue 17	During black-out *Lengthy crash*	(Page 55)
Cue 18	To open SCENE 11 *Thin wind blows*	(Page 58)
Cue 19	**Christine:** "No." *Fade out wind*	(Page 59)
Cue 20	The **Phantom** jumps from the statue *Restore wind at high level*	(Page 63)
Cue 21	The **Phantom** throws **Old Man** off roof *Cut wind*	(Page 63)

ACT II

Cue 22	**The Persian:** "I'm going to pull it." Music *Creaking sound*	(Page 79)
Cue 23	To open SCENE 4 *Dry ice, mist. Water dripping. Echo effect*	(Page 80)
Cue 24	Song 12 begins *Fade out drips*	(Page 81)
Cue 25	To open SCENE 5 *Drifting smoke. Loud hum. Echo effect*	(Page 82)
Cue 26	**The Persian** drags **Mauclair** off, R *Fade boiler hum*	(Page 84)

Cue 27   To open Scene 6   (Page 88)
             Water drips

Cue 28   **Raoul** moves to c   (Page 88)
             Rat effect

Cue 29   **Raoul** drops a coin and listens. After an interval   (Page 88)
             Distant plop

Cue 30   **Raoul** moves onstage a couple of paces   (Page 88)
             Sharp whipping sound

Cue 31   **Raoul:** " And turn the key" Long pause   (Page 92)
             Sound of a bolt and massive grinding of stone

Cue 32   **The Persian:**(*off, softly*) "... getting somewhere."   (Page 92)
             Twittering of birds

Cue 33   **Raoul:** "Iron!" Music rumbles   (Page 94)
             Birds become distorted

Cue 34   **The Persian:** "Six. And six of us"   (Page 94)
             Great screech of metal

Cue 35   **The Phantom:** "Adieu." Music has died   (Page 95)
             Soft hissing, building in intensity

Cue 36   Song 15 begins   (Page 96)
             Fade out hissing

Cue 37   Song 15 ends   (Page 99)
             Hissing building to a loud level over scene change

Cue 38   Snap to black-out   (Page 103)
             Wooden thump of an opening trapdoor. A thump